Tears Of A Hustler 3

A Novel By

Silk White

Good2GoPublishing

Published by:
GOOD2GOPUBLISHING
7311 W. Glass Lane
Laveen, AZ 85339
www.good2gopublishing.com
facebook/silkwhite
twitter @silkwhite
silkwhite212@yahoo.com
Ravon@good2gopublishing.com

ThirdLane Marketing: Brian James
Brian@good2gopublishing.com

Cover design: Davida Baldwin
Edited by: M.S.Hunter
ISBN: 978-0-578-08474-9

Typesetter: Rukyyah

Tears of a Hustler 2
Flashback

Chapter 40
Fight Night

"How you feeling baby?" Rodney asked in an exciting voice.

"I feel good," The Terminator replied as he sat in the locker room getting his hands wrapped up.

"All you gotta do is go out and do it just like we did it in the gym and you won't have any problems tonight," Mr. Wilson assured his fighter.

"I'm going to make you look good tonight," TheTerminator said, winking at his trainer.

"I want a lot of head movement. Because when The Bully hits, he hits hard," Mr. Wilson raised an eyebrow.

"Come on, I know you don't think this chump can beat me?" The Terminator asked, clearly ffended.

"I never said that," Mr. Wilson countered. "All I'm saying, is to keep your head moving so you don't get caught with a big shot."

"I'm too smooth to lose and I'm too quick to get hit," The Terminator said as he stood up and began working on his foot work.

"This gon be a good ass fight," Eraser Head said as he backed his Range Rover into a parking spot and let the engine die.

"I don't care who wins. I just want to see somebody get knocked the fuck out," G-money slurred as he slid out of the vehicle. "Damn I'm twisted right now," he admitted.

"I'm kinda saucey too," Eraser Head said, with a hint of Grey Goose still on his breath.

"Be a good ass fight," Pauleena said out loud as she and Malcolm took their seats.

"Yes this is going to be entertaining," Malcolm agreed.

"It better be," Pauleena said as she saw G-money and

Eraser Head headed in her direction.

"What's good ma, how you feeling?" G-money said, walking past Malcolm like he was invisible, as he hugged Pauleena tightly. As he hugged Pauleena, he purposely brushed his hand across her ass. "Let's go half on a baby," he whispered in her ear.

Pauleena laughed out loud. "I give you some of this pussy and I'll have you working for free."

"The way you looking in that grey dress, I wouldn't mind working for free," G-money said seriously.

"You been drinking?" Malcolm butted in.

G-money looked at the big man, but didn't answer. "Who told this chump he can talk?" He said, looking at Pauleena.

"Leave Malcolm alone," Pauleena said as she sat back down and saw a familiar face on the other side of the arena sitting in the crowd. "Look at these clowns," she nudged Gmoney.

When G-money looked up, he saw Romelo and his bodyguard sitting about three rows away from the ring. Seconds later, Pauleena and G-money saw Marvin, Smitty, and Moonie snake their way threw the crowd making their way towards Romelo and Tango.

"Yo, ain't that shorty you was about to get into it with at Romelo's house?" G-money asked, pointing at Moonie.

"Yeah that's that bitch," Pauleena said in an uninterested tone.

"What's good? You want me to go over there and slap that bitch for you?" G-money asked seriously.

"Nah, she get a pass just this one time," Pauleena told him.

The Bully stood in his dressing room, with his trainer and entourage, warming up.

"I want you to go out there and pinch a whole in this guy's face," The Bully's trainer told him.

"I got this Walter," The Bully said confidently as he bounced up and down.

"The ref is here," one of his boys called out.

"Let him in," The Bully yelled.

"Good luck tonight," the ref said as he shook The Bully's hand. "Listen, I know you two don't like each other, but I don't want no foul play, no elbows, and keep them punches up, am I understood?"

"I got you," The Bully answered as he sat down so he could get his hands wrapped up.

"Do you have any questions?"

"Yeah, make sure when I unload on that bitch, he don't be grabbing me and all that," The Bully told him.

The new all black S5 Audi pulled into a parking spot bumping 50 cents song "I Like The Way She Do It".

Rell slid out of the driver seat wearing a royal blue L.A. Dodger fitted, a white thermal shirt, some black jeans, and a pair of old royal blue Pennies. A bad white bitch slid from the back seat and stood by his side, along with one of his shooters. When Rell stepped foot in the arena, he lit the place up like Las Vegas with all the jewelry he wore. He had on at least three chains, an iced out watch, and a foolish bracelet.

"Where are our seats?" The pretty green eyed woman asked.

"Way down in the front," Rell answered quickly as he threw on his shades and lead the way.

"I wish these niggaz would hurry up and fight already," G-money huffed.

"They should be coming out any minute," Pauleena said out loud.

"Get the fuck outta here," Eraser Head said out loud as he nudged G-money with his elbow.

"What up?" G-money said, turning to face Eraser Head.

"Look over by the second row," Eraser Head said, pointing.

"What am I looking for?" G-money said, still searching the crowd.

"Look at the nigga with the blue hat on," Eraser Head said, still pointing.

When G-money finally realized who Eraser Head was pointing to, he quickly shot to his feet.

"Chill, chill. We gon handle this nigga as soon as the fight is over," Eraser Head said, holding G-money back with one arm.

"Who's that?" Pauleena asked curiously.

"Rell," G-money answered with fire dancing in his eyes.

"Who, that corny looking nigga with the white bitch?" Pauleena asked, making sure they were talking about the same person.

"Yeah he's a dead man walking," G-money said as all the lights in the arena went out. Seconds later, they began flashing as The Bully made his way towards the ring. Over on the other side of the arena, sat Frank along side him was Jimmy.

"Hey Frank what's up with that moolie Gmoney?"

"What about him?" Frank asked as he stood up and cheered for The Bully.

"He's sitting over there on the other side. You want me to take him when he goes outside?" Jimmy asked in a calm tone.

"Nah, I'm over that. Let the moolie live," Frank told him.

"Let's go out here and get this done champ," Mr. Wilson yelled in The Terminator's ear as the two made their way to the ring. "Work your jab and you'll have an easy night."

The Terminator just nodded his head, signaling he understood as Rodney swiped a fans hand off The Terminator's robe as he jogged up the steps to the ring. Once both fighters were in the ring, the crowd went
crazy in anticipation of what they were about to witness.

"It's show time baby," The Bully's trainer yelled aggressively as he applied Vaseline to his fighter's face. "This is what you been working for your whole life. Don't let nobody or nothing take this from you, you hear?"

The Bully nodded his head yes as he stared down The Terminator over in the other corner. He was completely in the zone.

"Both fighters to the center of the ring please," the referee called. "Okay I've spoke to both of you in the back already. I want a nice, clean fight. This is good," he said, pointing to both men belt lines. "Anything lower, is no good. Do ya'll have any questions?" Both fighters shook their heads no, at the same time.

"Okay good luck to both of ya'll. Touch gloves," the referee said as the two fighters touched gloves, and headed to their separate corners.

"This first round I want you to work that jab," Mr. Wilson said in The Terminator's ear as he rubbed his shoulders. "The jab will set everything up," he said one last time as he exited the ring.

Once the bell sounded, the crowd erupted as the two fighters met in the middle of the ring. The Bully started the fight off with a powerful jab, followed by a right hand. The powerful blows bounced off The Terminator's gloves as he danced out of the way.

The Terminator took a couple of steps backwards so he could get a good look at how The Bully kept his guard up. Just by looking at the man's defensive stance, he knew off the back he could hit him with at least two or three different punches, easy.

As The Bully came charging in, The Terminator took a quick step back and threw a swift left hook that landed on the side of The Bully's head. The punch caused The Bully's face to move, but the blow didn't seem to phase him, as he continued to come straight forward.

"Stop running like a little bitch!" The Bully taunted.

The Terminator just smiled as he threw two stiff jabs and danced out of the way before the two could exchange blows.

"Stop running and fight!"

The Bully growled as he cut off the ring and managed to catch The Terminator close to the ropes. As soon he saw an opening, he took it. The Bully threw three vicious hooks upstairs, then went downstairs and threw four punches to the body. The Terminator stood in his Philly shell defensive stance as he blocked most of the punches with his gloves and shoulder. As The Bully continued to charge straight ahead, The Terminator caught him with two quick straight right hands, as the bell sounded, ending the first round.

"Get this man some water!" The Bully's trainer yelled as he shoved a long Q-tip up The Bully's nose. "Let me get a deep breath. This motherfucker don't want to fight, so you going to have to bring the fight to him. Keep going straight at him, just keep your head moving at all times," he told him.

"You see what I see out there champ?" Mr. Wilson asked as he squirted some water in The Terminator's mouth.

"What's that?" The Terminator asked, taking a deep breath.

"This guy is a sucker for counter punches, so I want you to stop all that sticking and moving bullshit. Stand in there with that chump and pick your punches. He's open all day. Let's make it happen," Mr. Wilson said in a regular tone as the bell rung, signaling the start of round two.

The Terminator started the round off with two stiff jabs. The Bully side stepped one of them and fired back with a left hook, and a straight right hand. The two shots caught The Terminator off guard, causing him to stumble off the impact. The Bully followed up with another left hook. The punch missed, but the tip of his elbow connected with the corner of The Terminator's eye. The Terminator danced out the way and instantly felt the warm blood trickling down his eye. He pawed away as much blood as he could with his glove, as he saw The Bully continue to come forward. The Terminator threw a quick jab, followed by a right hook to the body before dancing out of range, pawing at his eye again.

"Stop running you little bitch!" The Bully taunted again as he blocked a jab and hook with his gloves, and fired back with a hard, straight right hand that landed in the middle of The Terminator's face, as the bell sounded.

The Terminator headed back to his corner and Mr. Wilson was all over him. "What the hell are you waiting for?" He barked.

"He's cheating!"

"I don't want to hear shit about no cheating," Mr. Wilson yelled as he splashed some water in The Terminator's face.

"Stop waiting and go get it in," he yelled as the cut man did his best to stop The Terminator's eye from bleeding.

"I hurt that bitch!" The Bully said with an evil smirk on his face.

"That clown can't fight," The Bully's trainer said out loud as he applied Vaseline to his fighter's face.

"Keep going straight at him. He's going to break down in the later rounds watch," he told The Bully as the bell rung.

At the start of round three, the two fighters met in the middle of the ring again. The Terminator started things off landing two out of three jabs.

"That's all you got bitch?" The Bully snarled as he bobbed his head from side to side, and fired a jab of his own.

The Terminator quickly stepped back and countered the jab with a sharp left hook, followed by a straight right hand. The hook landed perfectly on The Bully's jaw, causing his mouth piece to fly out his mouth, while the straight right hand dazed him a little bit. Once The Terminator saw that he had The Bully hurt, he went in for the kill; throwing punches from all angles, causing the crowd to rise to their feet. Once the punches started raining in, The Bully quickly grabbed The Terminator's arms and held on for dear life.

"Get the fuck off me!" The Terminator growled as he snuck in an upper cut, while the referee separated the two.

"Come on bitch. That's all you got?" The Bully slurred as he backed up into the corner.

The Terminator threw a quick jab that snapped The Bully's head back, then threw a six punch combination as the bell sounded ending the round.

"That's what I'm talking about. Just use your head and you got this fight in the bag!" Mr. Wilson yelled as he squirted some water in The Terminator's mouth.

"What the fuck are you doing out there?" The Bully's trainer yelled as he splashed water in his fighter's face.

"Turn this shit into a dog fight you hear?"

"I got you," The Bully replied as he stood for the next round.

At beginning of the next round, The Bully came out letting his hands fly. The Terminator stood in his Philly shell defensive stance as he blocked six of eight shots. He could tell by The Bully's movement and body language, that he was beginning to run out of gas. The Terminator landed six punches in rapid succession, before The Bully decided to fire back with a wild hook. The Terminator easily side stepped the hook and landed a sharp upper cut that wobbled The Bully. As The Bully felt his legs buckle, he knew he had to do something. As The Terminator came in for the kill, he threw a hard hook. The Bully managed to duck the hook by inches, and countered with an uppercut below The Terminator's belt, dropping him instantly.

"If you do that again, I'm taking a point!" The referee yelled as he pushed The Bully to an empty corner, while The Terminator laid on the floor clutching his family jewels.

"Come on champ, shake it off. You got five minutes to get yourself together," the referee told him, as the crowd continued to boo The Bully for the cheap shot.

Two minutes later, The Terminator was up walking around gingerly. "That nigga did that shit on purpose!" He yelled out to Mr. Wilson.

"Well whip his ass then!" Mr. Wilson yelled back.

"You ready to go?" the Ref asked excitedly.

"Yeah I'm ready!" The Terminator replied as he and The Bully met up in the middle of the ring again. The Bully threw two jabs followed by a hook. The Terminator ducked the hook and came up with a vicious uppercut that dropped The Bully straight on his face.

Once The Terminator saw The Bully hit the canvas face first, he knew he wasn't getting up. The ref made it to the count of 10 easily.

"That's what I'm talking about," Mr. Wilson sang happily as he jumped in The Terminator's arm.

"Can't nobody beat you! You the fucking man!" Rodney yelled as he lifted The Terminator up on his shoulders.

"I'm out," G-money said as he kissed Pauleena on the cheek.

"Where you going?" She asked in a worried voice.

"I gotta go handle some business," he replied, nodding in Rell's direction.

Pauleena didn't respond. She just kissed G-money on his cheek and hugged him tightly. "Be careful," she whispered in his ear.

"I got you ma," G-money told her as he and Eraser Head spun around and headed in Rell's direction.

"Fuck!" Eraser Head yelled. Rell had somehow managed to blend in with the crowd.

"I called the goons, they outside. No way he should get pass them," G-money said as he and Eraser Head took hurried steps towards the exit.

"Keep your head and eyes open," Rell said to his shooter as he held on to blue eye's arm.

"I got you," the shooter replied as he spit the street razor that he had stashed in the side of his gums, into the palm of his hand.

"Yo go grab the ride. Me and Brittany gon wait right here," Rell said, tossing his young shooter the keys. "Hurry the fuck up too," he said, looking over both shoulders.

Rell knew that nobody was strapped in Madison Square Garden. That's why he chose to stay there until his young boy pulled up front. If anybody ran up on him, he could handle a fist fight. As Rell and Brittany stood in the lobby, Rell noticed three suspicious looking guys strolling around the parking lot. Something about the men just screamed trouble. Loco, Gun Play, and a Y.G. (young gansta) from the hood
strolled through the parking lot looking for Rell.

"Yo, what this nigga look like again?" Gun Play asked.

"I don't know. Eraser Head said money got braids and a royal blue hat on, with mad chains on," Loco said out loud.

"Man, we ain't gon never find this nigga!" Gun Play snapped.

"Come on lets go!" Rell said when he saw his shooter pull up front.

"Money right there got on a blue hat, and mad chains," Gun Play said, pointing at the man and white woman sliding in the Audi. Gun Play thought about popping off, but the two police officers walking around, cancelled that idea.

"These niggaz know better than to try something down here on 34th street," the shooter said with a smirk as he pulled off with his .45 sitting on his lap.

As the Audi pulled off, Rell saw G-money and Eraser Head exit the building. For a split second,
the two made eye contact. Each man, giving the other a murderous glare.

"That was that clown right there," G-money said as he watched the Audi peel out of the parking lot.

"Come on. If we hurry, we can catch that pussy!" Eraser Head said as the two raced to the car.

The Audi came to a stop directly on the side of an all black van on a low key block.

"Baby take the car home and I'll see you later," Rell told her as he and his shooter exited the Audi and slid in the van. Once inside the van, the two men traded their night clothes for
black jeans, black sweat shirts.

"Tonight we going hunting," Rell said as he loaded his Mox-berg shotgun with the pistol grip. "You ready to get your feet wet," he asked, looking at his shooter for a response.

"Only one way to find out," the youngster said confidently.

"We ain't gon never find this motherfucker," Eraser Head said in a lazy drawl, as he cruised down block after block looking for the all black Audi. G-money jiggled the white foam cup he was holding
before taking a sip.

"He's hiding like a little bitch. Fuck it; let's go hit up the club. I'm tired of looking for this chump," G-money said dryly.

Eraser Head noticed that G-money hadn't been himself for the past two weeks. "Yo, you a'ight?" He asked in a concerned tone.

"Yeah, I'm good," G-money answered, showing a weak smile. "I just feel like my man Mitch, from Paid in Full right now. I need to be around some love tonight, smell me?"

"I got you. I know the perfect spot," Eraser Head said as he made a sudden detour.

Chapter 41
Party Time

Alfonzo stood outside on 31st, between 7th and 8th Ave, in front of club Rebel. He loved working security at the night club cause for one, he got to look at beautiful women all night. And two, he got paid to look at beautiful women all night. Things couldn't of been going better for Alfonzo, until he saw G-money walking towards the front entrance with five goons behind him.

"Alfonzo, what's good?" G-money said as he gave the bouncer dap.

"Ain't nothing good," Alfonzo said folding his arms. "You know you banned from this club."

"Banned?" G-money echoed. "Banned for what?"

"Remember a while back, you and a couple of your buddies came in here and almost stomped a guy to death?" Alfonzo said, refreshing G-money's memory.

"Come on B. That shit happened like a year ago," G-money pointed out.

"Don't matter how long ago that was, the guy sued the club. So therefore, you and your peoples are banned from this club," Alfonzo said like it was his club.

G-money sucked his teeth. "Yo nobody asked you all that. You letting us in the club or not?"

"I already told you no!" Alfonzo said way louder than he had to, trying to impress a few chicks who stood in the front of the line.

"A yo fam, what's really good?" Loco stepped up. "We just want to have a good time tonight. Why you fronting for?"

"Listen new jack," Alfonzo began. "I don't even know you, so why are you even talking to me?"

Loco sighed loudly as he turned and snuffed Alfonzo, sending him stumbling back towards the entrance. Before he knew what was going on, Gun Play and two other goons were on the bouncer like a pack of wolves.

G-money and Eraser Head just sat back watching Loco and his goons put it in.

"I like this guy already," G-money said with a smile.

"Me too," Eraser Head added as he continued to look on.

Seconds later, five big bouncers came running towards the fight, but they quickly came to a halt when Gun Play backed out his .357. "Back the fuck up," he growled as he waved the cannon back and forth. "We out," he yelled as Loco and the other two goons all took off running back to their car.

"Be out, there go five-o," G-money yelled.

Gun Play quickly took off running down the block. Before he bent the cover, he made sure he tossed the burner down a sewer drain.

"Are these men giving you problems?" Four uniform cops asked as they walked up.

"Yeah get them out of here!" Alfonzo growled, pointing at G-money and Eraser Head.

"Okay come on fella's lets get going," one of the officers said as he grabbed G-money's arm.

"Do me a favor...don't put ya hands on me!" G-money said as he jerked his arm loose.

"Make a move!" The officer snarled getting all up in G-money's face.

"Come on, we out. Fuck these crackers," Eraser Head said as he pulled G-money away. "They only tough when it's a lot of them anyway," he waved the officer's off.

"Get somebody up here to shoot this bitch up!" G-money ordered.

"I got some goons on their way up here now. They should be close by," Eraser Head as he pulled out his cell phone and dialed a number. On the forth ring, a deep voice man answered.

"Yeah what's up?"

"Yo junior, where you at?" Eraser Head asked.

"I'm right around the corner from the club. It's popping in there?"

"Fat motherfucker at the front door fronting. I need you to send a little message."

"Say no more I got you," Junior said as he ended the call.

"It's done," Eraser Head said, flipping close his phone.

"Let's get up outta here before I have to wash somebody up," (beat them up) G-money huffed as he slid in the passenger side of the Benz. Once inside the vehicle, he grabbed some ice from out of the bag in the back seat and dropped a few cubes in his foam cup, before filling it up with Hennessy.

"Its any left for me?" Eraser Head asked as he slid behind the wheel.

"Yeah its cups and ice in the back," G-money told him.

Eraser Head fixed him a quick drink, then pulled out into traffic.

A block away, Rell sat in the all black van, along with his young soldier. "You ready to do this?"

The young shooter placed his Mac 11 on his lap and nodded his head yes.

"Lets ride out," Rell said from behind his ski mask.

The young shooter rolled his ski mask over his face, then pulled out into the street.

"I'mma go see Ali tomorrow," G-money said, staring blankly out the window.

"Word? You sure them crackers gon be cool with that?"

"Yeah, Mr. Goldberg said everything is cool."

"That's what's up," Eraser Head said as he made a left at the light. "Tell that nigga I said what up."

G-money nodded and sipped some more. "I got you."

"I gotta give it to him," Eraser Head began. "He been down for a minute and never said a word."

"That's what real niggaz do," G-money said as he noticed two PYT's (pretty young things) strolling down the block. "Yo pull over!"

The two ladies took a few steps away from the curb when they saw the Benz come to a sharp stop. "Damn, what the fuck?" A girl wearing a short jean skirt barked.

"My bad ma," G-money apologized as he grabbed his .45 from under the seat and tucked it in the small of his back, as he slid out the passenger seat. "Where the party at ladies?"

"We was on our way to Rebels," Jean skirt announced.

"Nah, we just came from there. Ain't nothing happening over there," G-money said as he leaned up against a parked car.

"You sure?" Jean skirt asked, flashing a smile.

"Its dead over there," Eraser Head said, adding himself into the conversation. "So what's good? Ya'll got names?"

"I'm Nicole," Jean skirt said, pointing to herself. "And this here is my girl Trice."

"I'm E and this is my man G-money," Eraser Head said, introducing the two.

"Yeah, this the club right here. Pull up at the end of the block," Junior ordered as he loaded his Desert Eagle. Once the driver pulled up at the end of the block, Junior slid out of the passenger seat with his gun hanging by his side. He counted to three in his mind before he raised his gun in the club's direction, and let off eight shots in rapid succession. As soon as the shots finished ringing out, Junior hopped back in the vehicle, not caring who he hit or if he had hit anybody at all. Once Junior was back in the vehicle, the driver quickly pulled off.

G-money sat leaning against the parked car talking to Nicole, when he heard some shots go off. From the sound of the shots, he could tell that the shots came from a few blocks away. Immediately, he looked over at Eraser Head and flashed a smirk.

"There them motherfuckers go right there," Rell said out loud as he rolled down his window, and aimed his shot gun at his target. Once the van got close enough, he pulled the trigger without hesitation.

As soon as the thunderous shot went off, G-money quickly tried to duck behind the parked car that he was leaning on, but he was a little too slow. Two pellets, from the shotgun, landed in the top part of his shoulder and collar bone. He quickly dropped down to the ground, pulling Nicole down with him.

"Yo ma, get down!" Eraser Head yelled as he grabbed Trice down behind the parked car, next to the one G-money and Nicole was hiding behind. He quickly pulled his 9mm from his waistband. "Yo, G, you a'ight?"

"I'm good!" G-money yelled back as he felt his warm blood running down his arm. "Ya'll niggaz wanna play?" He said out loud as he snatched his .45 from the small of his back with his good arm.

Rell hopped out the van and aimed his shot gun at the parked car that G-money stood behind, and pulled the trigger.

G-money and Nicole squatted behind the parked car as broken glass rained on top of their heads.

Rell and his young shooter slowly inched towards the parked car.

Once G-money heard the foot steps getting closer, he reached his arm over the hood of the car and let off three shots. Once those three shots went off, all hell broke loose.

Eraser Head quickly sprung from behind his hiding spot and began popping shots at the gunmen. When the young shooter saw Eraser Head spring up from behind the car, he aimed his Mac 11 at the man and pulled the trigger.

Once the machine gun went off, G-money quickly sprinted from behind the car, crouched over, letting his .45 bark. One of his bullets found a home in Rell's upper thigh, causing him to stumble backwards and lean up against the van for support.

When the young shooter saw G-money make his move, he swept his arm in G-money's direction and pulled the trigger. Two of the bullets from the Mac 11 ripped through the back of G-money's leg, dropping him in the middle of the street.

G-money hit the ground and looked up and saw Rell standing in the line of fire. Instantly, he raised his .45 and let off six shots in rapid succession. One of the bullets landed in Rell's neck, while the other five found homes in his chest, killing him instantly.

The young shooter looked over and saw Rell laid out in the middle of the street. Before he could turn his focus back on the target, a bullet ripped through his shoulder, causing him to drop his Mac 11. Not knowing what else to do, the young shooter sprinted down the street clutching his shoulder.

Eraser Head quickly reloaded his 9mm and began chasing the young shooter up the block.

"Fuck!" G-money cursed loudly as he laid in the middle of the street in a pool of his own blood. He winced in pain as he reached down in his pocket with his good arm, and pulled out a broken up blunt and lighter. "What a motherfucking day," he chuckled as he threw a piece of the blunt in his mouth and put fire to the end of it. He laid on the ground for about 45 seconds puffing on the blunt, until he heard a car come to a screeching stop and a familiar voice. "G-money is that you?" Carl asked as he rushed over to G-money's side.

"Some corny nigga got the drop on me," G-money said, flashing a weak smile.

"We gotta get you to a hospital!" Carl said as he lifted G-money's upper body into the car. G-money screamed in pain when Carl put his legs in the car.

"Sorry for getting blood on your seats," G-money apologized. "I'mma cop you a new whip when this shit is over."

"Don't even worry about it," Carl replied in a neutral tone.

"Yo, you got a phone on you?"

"Nah, I left my shit in the crib," Carl said in a shaky voice.
"Damn I wanted to call Coco and let her know what's going on," G-money said in obvious pain.

"I'll call her for you when we get to the hospital," Carl told him.

"Good looking my nigga," G-money said as he closed his eyes and tried to relax as Lil Wayne's song "Misunderstood" pumped through the speakers. Five minutes later, G-money opened his eyes to the sound of Carl's cell phone ringing.

"I thought you left your jack (phone) in the crib?" G-money asked suspiciously.

"Nah, this phone is pre-paid and it only got like one minute on it," Carl stuttered.

"Where the fuck we at?"

"We here right now," Carl said as he pulled in a dark alley.

G-money laughed out loud. "Youz a real bitch ass nigga," he said with a smirk on his face.

"No, I'm a real O.G." Carl said as he pulled out his .357 and aimed it at G-money's head. "You and ya boys been running around all wild and shit. I asked you a thousand times to just ask them to move from in front of my building with that bullshit, but I guess a hard head makes a soft ass."

"I could of twisted ya shit back in the lobby that day."

"That's the difference between ya'll young niggaz and a real O.G. We don't play," Carl snarled.

"So do what you gotta do then," G-money said, flashing his trademark smile. The last thing G-money saw was the muzzle on the .357 flash.

"Punk motherfucker!" Carl said as he slid out the vehicle, threw his hoody over his head, and headed down the block like nothing happen.

After chasing the young soldier five blocks, Eraser Head gave up. He quickly tossed his 9mm in the trash can, then headed in a totally different direction. Eraser Head made it about a half a block, when a Lincoln pulled up on the side of him. "Fuck!" He cursed as he kept on walking straight thinking it was the police riding up on him. A woman's voice caused him to stop and look. He breathed easy when he saw Nicole and Trice in the back seat of the cab. "Get in!" Trice yelled.

Eraser Head quickly slid in the back seat with the ladies as the cab driver quickly pulled off.

"I gotta go back and get my man!" Eraser Head said.

"Someone picked him up already," Trice told him.

"You sure?"

"Yeah some guy with a baby afro dragged him in his car," Nicole said, confirming the story.

"A'ight bet," Eraser Head said, feeling a little better inside. Before the cab driver dropped the ladies off, Eraser Head and Trice traded numbers. "I'mma call you probably tomorrow a'ight?"

"I'll be waiting," Trice replied flirtatiously as she and Nicole headed towards their building. Once the ladies were gone, Eraser Head gave the cab driver directions to Pauleena's house. On the ride, Eraser Head pulled out his phone and made a quick call.

Shorty stood in front of a building in the projects poppin shit with about six to eight other soldiers. "Yo what's good? Ya mom's cooked tonight?" He asked one of the soldiers.

"You tryna be funny, you little ugly motherfucker?" The soldier shot back as all the men around them fell out laughing.

"What? You know me and ya mom's go way back," Shorty laughed as he answered his vibrating boost phone. "What's the deal?"He answered.

Grab all the soldiers you can find and strap up. G-money just got shot. I'mma meet you at the spot in an hour," Eraser Head said, ending the call.

"Yo tell ya mom's she better have my slippers waiting at the door for me when I get home," the soldier continued as soon as Shorty got off the phone.

"Its on, G-money just got hit. Round up all the goons and have 'em meet me at the spot in an hour," Shorty ordered as he and three soldiers jogged to his car and peeled off.

Detective Nelson and Detective Bradley sat across the street in an unmarked car, watching Shorty's every move.

"I think we got something good!" Detective Nelson said excitedly as he watched Shorty and three of his soldiers jog to the car and pull off into traffic.

"I hope so, cause I'm tired of following this piece of shit around all fucking day," Detective Bradley huffed.

Shorty reached the stash crib and double parked on the corner, as he and the soldiers headed upstairs. Twenty minutes later, thedetectives noticed six cars pull up in front of the same building.

"I told you something big was going down tonight," Detective Nelson said with a smile as he watched the men head in the same building. He quickly pulled out his cell phone and called for back up.

"We about to go push these niggaz shit back!" Shorty said, holding a double barrel shotgun. Each man in the apartment was armed with more than one gun.

"Yo, I just got word back that it was Rell and his peoples," a soldier announced, reading a text message out loud.

"Fuck that! We going hunting," Shorty said out loud as he and all the soldiers exited the apartment. Once outside, each man hopped in the vehicle he came in. Before Shorty could switch the gear from park to drive, a cop car came to a screeching stop directly in front of his car. Seconds later, flashing lights were everywhere.

"Fuck!" Shorty cursed as he searched for an escape, but it was no use. Him and his whole crew were boxed in.

Chapter 42
I Don't Believe It

"Out of nowhere, bullets just started flying from everywhere," Eraser Head said, replaying the story.

"So where's G-money now?" Pauleena asked with a concerned look on her face.

"I have no idea," Eraser Head said with a hurt look on his face.

Pauleena quickly walked to the living room and turned the T.V. to the news.

"Breaking news: Gerald Williams, better known in the streets as G-money, was found dead tonight in a stolen car parked in an alley. Police are saying this murder is believed to be drug related. Also, tonight several men who worked for Williams were caught hours later with loaded fire arms. Police say Williams and his crew were at war with another crew over territory. We'll have more details as this story develops," the reporter said.

"Fuck!" Eraser Head cursed as the tears silently rolled down his eyes.

"Where the fuck were you when this happened?" Pauleena yelled, getting all up in Eraser Head's face as tears rolled down her face.

"I was chasing one of the niggaz who shot him," he told her as she burried her head in Eraser Head's chest.

"Don't worry. We gonna find the niggas who did this," Roy said, "just fucked up that most of the soldiers just got knocked." (locked up)

"I told Shorty to wait until he heard from me to make a move," Eraser Head raved. "Motherfuckers don't never listen!"

"Ahww hell naw," Knowledge said in a defeated tone as he watched the news from his living room in Philly. "Why all the bad shit gotta happen to the real niggaz?" He asked himself as he shook his head in disgust. At times like this, Knowledge wished he was still in the game. Deep down inside, he felt that if he was with G-money when it went down, he would still be alive.

Tears
Of
A Hustler
3

A NEW BREED

"Damn that shit is crazy" Marvin said shaking his head as he and his crew sat listening to the reporter. He never thought G-Money would go out the way he did, and especially so soon, but he couldn't say he wasn't happy about it. The drug game was a cut throat business and only the strong survived.

"At least he had a couple of years to enjoy all that money he made", Smitty said looking on with the rest of the crew. In his heart he was happy that now they wouldn't have to go head up with G-Money, with him out of the way things would become much easier. "So what's next?"

"We gonna take over all of G-Money's old spots and get it poppin" Marvin said with a smirk on his face.

"What about Pauleena?" Smitty asked.

"Fuck that bitch! Either she run with us or get ran the fuck over!" Marvin answered quickly. "If we want something we going to have to take it"!

"That's what I'm talking about," Moon said excitedly. "It's about time. I never liked that bitch anyway. What has she done to deserve her spot? She probably won't even bang out for her shit."

"Well we are definitely about to find out" Marvin said out loud as he turned off the TV. He was the leader, so he knew if anything went wrong it would all be landing on his shoulders, therefore Marvin knew he had to have his shit tight before he went after the crown, and failing wasn't an option.

Tears of a Hustler 3

"PLAN B"

"This shit is crazy" Pauleena said helping herself to a drink. "I should of just told you and G-Money to come back to the crib with me" she said looking over at Eraser Head. Deep down she had a feeling something bad was going to happen, and if she could change the hands of time she would.

"Everything happens for a reason" Eraser Head said downing a shot of Henny in one gulp. "The good die young." He shook his head.

"So what now?" Roy asked from the sideline.

"Shit doesn't stop" Pauleena said turning to face Eraser Head. "It's your turn to step up to the plate. You think you ready for that?"

"I was born ready" Eraser Head replied with a look that said you can't be serious. "Imma call a little meeting tomorrow. Inform all the soldiers and let them know what's going on."

"A'ight, cool. I know you a little short on muscle, so if anybody get out of line just holla at Roy" Pauleena told him. "I know you used to be G-Money's muscle but now you going to have to fall back cause once word get out that you the man, it's gon be a lot of eyes on you and we definitely can't have you out here running around like some wild cowboy," she told him. Pauleena really wanted to give the position to Roy, but Eraser Head knew his way around the city better than, so he got the job.

"I understand" Eraser Head began quietly. "I learned a lot from G-Money."

"I hope so," Pauleena said as tears still sat on the rim of her eyes, she missed G-Money and wished that she would of made him leave the fight with her instead of alone. "As soon as you hear anything on the motherfucker who did this to G-Money, you let me know."

"I got you. Imma go holla at shorty later on tonight and see what's good." He paused. "Matter of fact, I'mma get on that right now" Eraser Head said as he kissed Pauleena on the cheek then headed out the door.

Pauleena waited for Eraser Head to leave before she spoke to Roy. "Now that G-Money is gone, shit is about to get real ugly out here. Everybody in the city is going to be gunning for our spot"

"How you want to handle it?" Roy asked down for whatever.

"Not sure yet" Pauleena said. "Let's see how it plays out first, then plan from there" she told him.

Roy nodded his head, but he knew how his boss got down, so he knew a lot of blood was definitely about to get spilled, especially once they found out who was responsible for G-Money's murder.

"What's on your mind?" Pauleena asked.

"Just getting myself mentally prepared for what's about to go down" Roy smiled.

* * *

"You heard about your man G-Money?" Gunplay asked as he sat on the bench next to Loco and a few other local knuckleheads.

"Yeah that shit is fucked up" Loco said looking up and down the block for any sign of police. "Gotta be on point at all times!"

"You heard anything from Eraser Head yet?"

"Nope!" Loco replied quickly.

"Who you think going to take over now that G-Money is gone?" Gunplay asked, his mind was already scheming, and plotting on a quick come up.

"Don't care" Loco said simply as a local crackhead strolled up to the benches.

"Hey man you holding?" The fiend asked looking like he ain't had a hit in a day or two.

"Yeah right in the building" Loco said as he watched the fiend shuffle towards the building. "Get on that!" He said to his young worker who sat at the end of the bench. As soon as those words left his mouth he felt his cell phone vibrating on his waistline. He looked at the screen and saw Eraser Head's name flashing across the screen. "What's good?" He answered.

"Meeting tonight at a new spot. You'll receive a text message in about five minutes with the address. It starts at seven. Don't be late." Eraser Head said hanging up in Loco's ear.

"What was that about?" Gunplay asked curiously.

"Eraser Head just hit me up. He said it's a meeting tonight at seven."

"But I thought we were doing our own thing now since G-Money is gone," Gunplay said.

"We are. You think I just copped two hundred and fifty grams for nothing?" Loco chuckled as he watched two more fiends head in the building. "Everybody had their chance to eat while I was locked up, now it's my turn."

WHAT YOU GONNA DO"

Santana stood in front of his building talking to an around the way chick that he knew for years. "Come on ma don't act like that" he said trying to convince her to let him use her crib as a stash house.

"I ain't acting like nothing" Natalie said sucking her teeth. "I ain't messing with you like that."

"I just need you to keep a lil something in your crib for me, only for about a week" he pressed flashing his perfect smile.

"Nah, you wilding. Last time I did that you had your man Mac Mittens banging on my door at 4:30 in the morning" Natalie said fanning him off.

"That was different. This time I'm going to pick the shit up from you myself" Santana told her. "Please?"

For some reason Natalie could never tell Santana no. Maybe it was because she had a crush on him for years. Santana stood about 5'11 and weighed about 150 pounds. His light complexion and long braids that rested at the middle of his back is what seemed to keep the ladies loving him. "So are you gonna help me?" Santana asked as he licked his lips.

"Yeah I'm gon help you" Natalie said as she sucked her teeth. "You get on my nerves."

"You know you can't tell the gorgeous gangsta no."

"The gorgeous who?"

"You heard me" Santana said laughing out loud.

"Child please!" Natalie said shaking her head. Santana was about to reply until he noticed the all black Yukon pull up directly in front of his building. "Imma holla at you later a'ight?" Santana said as he kissed Natalie on the cheek.

"Okay call me later" Natalie said as she walked off throwing a little extra on her walk. Little did Santana know but, if he wanted Natalie's help he was going to have to dish out some dick this go around.

Once Natalie had walked off, Santana reached down in his back pocket and gripped the .380 that rested there as he posted up in front of the building waiting to see what was up.

Moonie slid out the driver's seat wearing a pair of tight fitting jeans, some pumps, and a wife beater. She rocked a long straight weave that came down to the middle of her back while the front was cut into a bang. She kind of favored the rapper Remy Martin.

"Santana, what's popping?" Moonie asked as she walked up.

"Ain't nothing popping" He snarled as he pulled out his .380.

"We not here for that" Smitty said as he stepped out the passenger seat of the Yukon. "That pistol won't be necessary, unless you want to die"

"You ain't done nothing with that shit anyway" Moonie added with a smirk on her face. She didn't care for Santana, and hoped that he made a move.

"What y'all think I'm stupid? I know what y'all be doing. Y'all not about to be extorting me" Santana said nervously, never backing down.

"We wanna talk business" Smitty told him.

"What kind of business?" Santana asked lowering his gun.

"Listen man," Moonie began. "We about to start taking over this whole shit and we want you to be a boss and run this other spot we got downtown, either you in or you out. If you in you get to make money, if not you already know what's gon happen."

"What about the spot that I got right here?"

"You didn't hear what she just said?" Smitty huffed. "Marvin is taking over everything. Either you can roll with us and make a lot of money or you can try to play the tough guy role and see how far that shit gets you."

"Nah I ain't no tough guy but don't get it twisted, I ain't no chump either." Santana said confidently. "I'm all about that kitty (money) so if you telling me that I can make more money than I'm making now, then count me in," he said as he gave Smitty a pound.

"Smart man" Smitty said. "And trust me you about to be making more money then you ever seen in your life"

* * *

"I'm so glad you all could make it" Eraser Head said, speaking to a room full of hustlers and goons. "I know you've all heard what happened to G-Money. Now that leaves me in charge." He announced. "Long story short, nothing is going to change. We are going to keep things running as smoothly as normal. Any questions?"

No one spoke.

"A'ight this meeting is over." Eraser Head announced as he and Roy made their exit.

"Why didn't you tell him that we wanted out?" Gunplay asked him as he and Loco made their way outside.

"Time and place for everything" Loco replied as the two slid in his 1999 BMW.

***

Loco found a parking spot by the side of his building. As usual, the projects were live with activity.

"Where we headed, towards the benches?" Gunplay asked pulling out a pack of Newport's.

"Nah, imma catch up with you later. Imma head upstairs for a minute" Loco said as he gave Gunplay a pound and headed towards his building. Loco stepped foot in the apartment and saw Monique sitting on the couch polishing her toe nails. She had her hair wrapped up in a scarf and had on a pair of boy shorts and a wife beater. "Where the fuck you been?" she asked not bothering to look up from her toes.

"Out taking care of some business," Loco told her.

"With one of your bitches?" Monique said still not taking her eyes off her toes. Loco let out an aggravated breath as he headed to the bedroom. "That chick got issues" He said to himself as he undressed for the shower.

"What the fuck you think you doing?" Monique asked busting in the room. She didn't like how Loco had tried to brush her off.

"About to take a shower," Loco replied looking at Monique like he just finished drinking some spoiled milk.

"You must think I'm stupid," Monique said snatching Loco's towel from out of his hand. "Why you taking a shower as soon as you walk in the door?"

"Because I can," Loco snatched his towel back.

"You was out fucking one of these dirty ass bitches wasn't you?" She asked folding her arms across her chest.

"What does it matter? We're not together anymore. The agreement was that you would let me stay here until I got back on my feet" Loco reminded her.

"Well fuck that, it's time for a new agreement," Monique said snaking her neck, stepping in front of Loco's path. "If you want to stay here, than you better be giving me some dick."

"Can I take a shower now?"

"Not just yet," Monique whispered as she pulled Loco's boxers down and slowly slid to her knees. Once face to face with Loco's already hard dick, she grabbed it with two hands and began licking and sucking on the head. Monique then licked up and down Loco's shaft until she reached his balls. She gently licked and sucked on each ball, then went back up towards the head. Once Loco's dick was thoroughly lubricated, Monique took the whole thing in her mouth and bobbed her head at a fast pace, the whole time making loud slurping noises until Loco exploded in her mouth.

"Now you can go take a shower" Monique yelled over her shoulder as she headed back to the living room.

Loco stood directly under the shower head in deep thoughts. The first thing he had to do was find a new place to stay, he knew if he stayed with Monique any longer he would wind up beating the shit out of her, so to avoid all that unnecessary drama, he was just going to leave as soon he found a new place to rest his head. Until then he would have to put up with Monique's shit.

"I Remember You"

Eraser Head slid out his Lexus, pulled out his cell phone and dialed a number. On the fifth ring a woman answered the phone.

"Hello?"

"Hello can I speak to Trice?"

"This is she."

"What up? This is E. I'm in front of your building. Which apartment you said you lived in again?"

"5 C"

"A'ight I'll be up in a minute" Eraser Head said ending the call. By the time he stepped off the elevator, Trice was already standing in her doorway waiting for him with a smile on her face.

"Had to make sure nobody tried to jump you or hit you over the top of the head before you made it up here," Trice joked as she gave Eraser Head a hug, then stepped to the side so he could enter. "It's about time you came by to see me. You want something to drink?"

"Nah I'm cool," Eraser Head replied as he watched Trice prance into the kitchen. She wore a mini skirt/dress kind of night gown with some furry slippers. "Do you still remember what that cat looked like who helped my man get in the car that night?"

"Yeah he was dark skinned and had some fuzzy braids" Trice said as she returned from the kitchen with a drink in hand. "Sure you don't want none of this Henny?"

"Nah I'm good ma" Eraser Head said holding up a palm. "You think if you saw the guy again you might be able to point him out?"

"Yeah" Trice began. "I got a good look at his face."

"Would you mind taking a ride with me down to the projects to see if we can find this guy?"

"Sure no problem, only under one condition," Trice said with a smile.

"What's that?" Eraser Head said returning her smile.

"You gotta take me out to dinner."

Eraser Head laughed out loud. "I got you ma."

"What's so funny?" Trice asked.

"I was actually going to take you out to dinner anyway," he told her.

"Even better" Trice said as she disappeared inside the bedroom. She returned wearing a pair of tight fitting jeans, a wife beater and some flip flops. Her hair was pulled back into a ponytail with a pair of Chanel sunglasses resting on top. "You ready?" She asked grabbing her cup of Hennessy from off the table.

"Yeah let's do this" Eraser Head replied as the two exited the apartment. Once inside the vehicle Trice sipped on Henny before she spoke. "So you think you know this guy with the braids?" She asked.

"Yeah I think it's this guy named Carl from the way you described him."

"So what is it that you need me to do?" Trice asked curiously.

"I just need you to knock on his door and act like you looking for a guy named Mike. He's going to tell you that you got the wrong apartment, but you really just knocking on the door so you can get a good look at his face." Eraser Head explained.

"I think I can handle that," Trice said and sipped some more. Eraser Head double parked on the side of Carl's building. "A'ight this the building right here."

"What apartment?" Trice asked, downing the last bit of her drink.

"8 F"

"A'ight I'll be back in a minute," Trice said as she headed over towards the building. Trice stepped off the elevator and searched for the "F" apartment. When she found it she quickly knocked on the door.

"Who is it?" A deep voice yelled from the other side of the door.

"It's me Candy," Trice yelled back as her voice echoed through the empty hallway. She heard a few locks unlock and saw a man peek his head through the door.

"Yeah what's up?" Carl asked looking Trice up and down.

"I'm new around here and somebody told me weed man lives here" Trice pulling out a crispy twenty dollar bill.

"Nah you got the wrong house. Don't no weed man stay here," Carl said with a disgusted look on his face.

"Oh I'm sorry." Trice said sincerely.

"No problem," Carl said as he went to close the door.

"Well do you know where I can get some bud from?" She asked before he fully closed the door.

"Nah I don't know anything about that," Carl told her before slamming the door in her face.

* * *

Eraser Head sat in the car with his eyes glued to the front of the building waiting for Trice to return. "What's taking her so long?" He thought out loud. He hoped Carl wasn't upstairs fucking her up. Seconds later, he saw Trice speed walking out of the building toward the vehicle.

"What's the word?" Eraser Head pressed.

"Yup, that's the same guy that helped your friend in the car." Trice announced hopping back in the passenger seat.

"I knew it," Eraser Head growled as he felt anger building up inside him. "Did he recognize you?"

"No, I don't think so."

"Very good" Eraser Head said as he handed Trice five hundred dollars.

"What's this for?" Trice asked holding up the bills.

"You earned that" Eraser Head replied as he pulled back out into traffic. Now that he knew who G-Money's killer was, it wouldn't be long until Carl got what was coming to him. From there Eraser Head decided to be nice and treat Trice to dinner for her hard work not to mention he was definitely feeling her.

"HARD TIMES"

"Can I come in?" Skip asked from the outside of Ali's cell. Every since G-Money had died Ali hadn't been himself.

"Yeah" Ali said breaking out of his daydream. "I can't believe my man is gone."

"I know, G-Money was my nigga too," Skip said in a weak voice. "You got any word on who did it?"

"Not yet," Ali answered as he stood up to stretch. "Whoever did it is on borrowed time." He knew the word would get out sooner or later and when it did, he knew G-Money's goons would definitely take care of it.

"You already know," Skip said as he and Ali exited the cell and walked over to the TV area. Even though Ali was out of the drug game, all the hustlers, killers, and stick up kids that called prison their home still respected him. He nodded his head acknowledging the few cats he dealt with.

"You heard anything from Loco?"

"Nah not yet," Ali replied. "I should be hearing from him soon though" he said as he heard the beefy C.O. calling his name. "Be right back," he told Skip as he headed over towards the bubble. (C.O. desk) "What up?"

"You got a visit. Your escort will be here in five minutes," the C.O. told him. "So be ready."

A huge smile spread across Nancy's face when she saw Ali walk through the visiting room door. "Who that?" Nancy asked little Ali pointing in

Ali's direction. She hadn't seen her man in a while and couldn't hide the excitement on her face.

"Dad dad" Little Ali said in a baby voice.

"Hey baby what's up?" Ali said as he scooped Little Ali up in his arms and kissed Nancy on the lips. He made sure he gave Lil Ali a big hug before he sat down.

"How you been holding up baby?"

"I can't complain," Ali replied as he sat Little Ali on his lap.

"So what's up? I got your letter in the mail talking about you had to talk to me face to face about something," Nancy said looking Ali dead in his face. Deep down she just prayed it wasn't anything bad.

Ali took one look at Nancy's pretty face and quickly looked away, he knew what he was about to drop on Nancy was sure to break and crush her heart.

"What?" Nancy said with a smile.

"I don't want to be with you anymore and I don't want you coming up here anymore either," he told her.

"What are talking about?" Nancy said with a confused look on her face. "What's this all about?"

"I don't want to be with you and I don't want you coming up here anymore." Ali repeated himself.

"Stop playing. I didn't come up here to play around," Nancy hoping this was all a sick joke.

"Does it look like I'm playing?" Ali said putting on his best poker face.

"Why? Where is this coming from?" Nancy whined. "I thought you loved me."

"Listen baby," Ali began quietly. "I do love you but it's not fair that your life has to stop because I made some bad decisions." He paused. "It's not fair to you, and I refuse to have you suffering because of my selfishness.

"Once you put that ring on my finger it's no longer about you, it's about us," Nancy shouted, causing her to get a few stares from the C.O.s. "I don't know what you are in here going through, but you better shake that shit off, because you must be crazy of you think I'm just going to leave you just because you are incarcerated!"

"You are still very young and it's so much you can be doing," Ali protested.

"Fuck that!" Nancy barked. "That's only an excuse!"

"I just feel like I'm holding you back smell me? You shouldn't have to live like this," Ali said looking away, he knew she wouldn't understand where he was coming from, but whether she liked it or not she could no longer come to visit him.

"I don't care what you say, I'll be up here on my regular schedule," Nancy said waiving Ali off.

"Listen you can come up here again but I'm going to deny the visit. Try me if you think I'm bullshitting," Ali simply stated.

"BABY WHY?"

"Live your life," he stood to his feet and handed Little Ali back to his mother. "Life is short, do better with your life then I did with mines"

"You are my life!" Nancy cried out. "Fuck that I'm not leaving you!"

Ali watched the tears roll down Nancy's face. "This life ain't for you," he said as he turned and headed towards the inmate exit.

"I'll wait for you!" Nancy yelled as she watched Ali walk out of the visiting room.

"NOT HAPPENING"

"Roy is here to see you," Malcolm said looking at Pauleena for a response.

"Let him in" Pauleena said from behind her desk as she helped herself to a shot.

Roy walked in Pauleena's office with a concerned look on his face. "We got problems."

"What's the problem?" Pauleena asked leaning back in her chair.

"Marvin!"

"Who the fuck is that?" Pauleena asked with an unconcerned look on her face. If she had never heard of him then he wasn't a problem. Besides Pauleena didn't deal with problems, she usually caused them.

"Romelo's son," Roy told her.

"What about him?" Pauleena shot back. She had heard of Romelo, and had even attended a few parties that he threw. The old school hustler seemed to be a good brother. To her knowledge, she thought she and Romelo were cool.

"This fuck nigga, been running around tryna take over all of G-Money's old spots!" Roy said in a southern drawl.

"G-Money's old spots?" Pauleena echoed. "I thought we had peoples on them corners?"

"We do. I mean we did." Roy said, shooting her a "you know what time it is" glance. "I say we go down there and tear shit up."

"Pass me that phone. Imma try to handle this like a business woman first," Pauleena said as she dialed Romelo's number.

***

Romelo sat in his living room looking at the worthless man that stood before him. A few people had begun to take his kindness for a weakness. "Where's my money?" Romelo asked in a calm voice.

"Come on you know I got you," Eric said with a nervous smile, inside he was scared to death. "We've been doing business for a minute."

"When you got me?" Romelo asked with a smirk.

"Why you tripping over a little $20,000? You know I always come through." Eric said defensively.

"Listen Eric you've been owing me that money for two months now. Stop playing with me," Romelo said with venom dripping from his tone. He had gave more than enough time to pay him back, now he was starting to feel like Eric was trying to disrespect him.

"Well what can I say? Things got a little slow," Eric said, shrugging his shoulders nonchalantly.

"Again, right?" Romelo said with a disbelieving look on his face. "Word on the streets is you just copped a new ride last week."

"Yeah, I thought I should treat myself to something nice you know?" Eric said with the shit face, right then and there he knew he had just fucked up.

"Yeah I know," Romelo said as he stood from behind his desk. "The problem is not what you owe, but how you owe. You don't go buy a new car when you owe somebody some money. It just doesn't look good."

"Nah, Romelo it's not even like that. You see what happened was..." Before Eric could finish his sentence, Tango had broken a pool stick over his back.

"Get up you little bitch!" Tango snarled as he grabbed him by the collar and yanked him back to his feet. "You one of them motherfuckers that think you slick right?" He asked with a menacing smile on his face. "I got something for bitches like you!"

"Come on man. Give me another chance." Eric begged. "I swear to God I'll get you your money!"

His cowardly plea was ignored. Tango wrapped his large hands around Eric's throat and began squeezing the life out of the man. He squeezed Eric's throat until the man's body stopped moving. "Little bitch!" Tango spat. "What you want me to do with this piece of scum?"

"Take him outside and put him in the trunk for now." Romelo ordered as he heard his cell phone ringing. "Pauleena?" He whispered to himself while looking at the Caller ID. "Hello?" He answered.

"I'm trying to reach Romelo."

"The one and only speaking." Romelo answered confidently.

"This is Pauleena. You and I need to talk."

"I'm all ears," Romelo said sitting back in his chair. He had ready heard what was going on, and was expecting his call.

"I been hearing that your son Marvin is on the come up." Pauleena said sarcastically.

"Okay so what's the problem?" Romelo said, getting to the point.

"The problem is he's trying to plant his seed on a few of my spots. Now I don't know if this was intentional, but if his people aren't moved within the next twenty four hours then I'm going to take it as an act of war!" Pauleena said meaning every word. "I didn't want to make a move on your son without speaking to you first out of respect."

"I feel where you're coming from."

"I mean that's just totally disrespectful. Normally I would have taken care of the situation, but when I heard it was your son I figured I would call you so things don't wind up getting out of hand." Pauleena told him.

"Thanks I appreciate that," Romelo said softly. "I don't know what's going on but I'm definitely going to talk to my son."

"Thank you," Pauleena said ending the call. Just from the sound of Romelo's voice she knew it was about to be a problem. From day one Pauleena always had to turn it up a notch, due to the fact that men didn't give the same type of respect as they would give a man, and that pissed her off.

"Everything alright boss?" Malcolm asked censing something wasn't right. He'd been working for Pauleena for a few years, and knew exactly when something wasn't right.

"These fucking clowns about to make me show my ass" Pauleena said downing a shot of Ciroc in one gulp. "They not trying to take me seriously, because I'm a female, and G-Money ain't here no more, but I got something for those mufucka's. If motherfuckers think they just gon push over on me they got another thing coming. I'm definitely getting down for this crown," Pauleena said out loud.

"I know that's right. I love it when you talk like that," Roy said as he raised his shot glass.

"Anybody who gets in our way is getting straight ran over, point blank!" Pauleena said slamming her fist down on the desk. "I don't give a fuck who it is!"

***

"You wanted to see me?" Marvin asked as he helped himself to a seat in his father's office.

"What's going on with you and that Pauleena girl?"

"Nothing," Marvin answered quickly.

"She just called me talking about you trying to take over a few of her spots." Romelo told him.

"Her crew ain't a hundred percent so I figured why not," Marvin said nonchalantly. He and his team were on the come up, and nobody was going to stop him from getting paid.

"You sure that's a smart business move? I mean, if y'all start beefing that could cause a lot of police action and that's not good for business." Romelo pointed out.

"Listen pops, I understand what you saying but I'm not standing around letting no girl call all the shots," Marvin continued. "How she controlling most of the real estate when she don't even be in the streets? I can't let that go down like that."

"I feel you. Just make sure you know what you doing. I heard out in Florida and Miami that she ain't to be messed with." Romelo warned.

"She ain't in Miami no more. This is New York. We definitely gonna see what she's all about, believe that," Marvin said with a smirk on his face. The stories he had heard about Pauleena were nothing but myth's to him, if she was really about something then she's definitely going to have to show him.

"It's your call, but if it was me I would just leave things how they are." Romelo told his son. "Don't be greedy, I've seen a lot of men get killed or tossed in a cell for being greedy."

"When G-Money had the streets on lock I didn't have a problem but a girl," Marvin paused. "Nah, not happening pops, you can talk until your face turns blue, ain't no bitch running the streets while I'm around....believe that!"

"Do what you gotta do then," Romelo said out loud, visualizing how the whole thing was about to play out in his mind and it wasn't a pretty site.

* * *

Nancy sat on the couch still wondering why Ali had just dropped her like that. "Was it another woman? Was he just tired of me? Was I doing something wrong?" She asked herself over and over again. She was confused, not only did she do every and anything Ali asked her, but on top of that she really loved him with all of her heart. A loud bang on the door caused her to jump. "Who is it?" She yelled once she reached the door.

"It's me bitch!"

Nancy immediately recognized the voice and opened the door.

"You look terrible," Coco said brushing past her best friend. "When was the last time you left this house?"

Nancy shrugged her shoulders. "I got everything I need right here in this house, beside what if Ali tries to call me? I'm definitely not going to miss that call."

"I know you not still tripping over that Ali shit?" Coco asked already knowing the answer. "You need to get over that shit already. It's his loss."

"You just don't understand what I'm going through right now." Nancy said as she broke down into tears.

"Listen Nancy, I just got over G-Money's death not too long ago," Coco paused. "I had to because I know he wouldn't have wanted me to be moping around all sad and shit, feel me?"

"I understand but it's going to take me a little longer to get over Ali," Nancy said, she had never had a man who treated the way he did, like the queen that she was. "I can't believe he told me not to come up there and see him no more."

"At least he set you up lovely. I mean you will never need a man for anything." Coco pointed out.

"It's not about the money. I really love that man. If it wasn't for him there's no telling where I would be right now." Nancy sobbed.

"I feel you but if he don't wanna see you then what are you going to do?"

"I don't know yet but I have to figure something out." Nancy replied.

"Well I'm going out tonight. You're more than welcome to join me if you'd like." Coco offered.

"Nah, imma just chill in the crib and get my thoughts together." Nancy said, all going out would do was have her out thinking about Ali, so she rather just play the crib for the night.

"Well if you change your mind, its going down tonight at Club Spotlight," Coco said as she kissed Nancy on the cheek and made her exit. She felt where her friend was coming from, but there was no way she would let a man that was locked up control her life.

"THE GORGEOUS GANGSTA"

Santana stepped foot out of his Dodge Magnum like he owned the world. He wore a wife beater up top, down low his Red Monkey jeans hung over his all black high top Prada shoes. He slid out the vehicle with a white foam cup in his hand. "What's goodie? How y'all niggas living?" He asked giving the local thugs, who always stood in front of the building, dap.

"Chilling," one of the thugs replied. "What you sipping on?"

"That gin and juice. You know I'm from the old school," Santana laughed as he strolled in the building. "Have that piff waiting on me when I get back!" he yelled over his shoulder. He jogged up to the third floor holding the big cross that hung around his neck down to his chest so it wouldn't bounce all over the place. He found the apartment he was looking for and did a special knock. Seconds later he door swung open and he disappeared inside.

"Damn, it's hot as fuck in here! Crack the window or something," Santana said out loud.

"Can't, Marvin said to keep these windows closed at all times," Shawn told him. Shawn was an old school hustler who had his own spot, but decided to let Marvin take it over only because the young man was offering him more money than he was making at the time.

"You got that bread ready for me?" Santana asked, ready to hurry up and make his exit. He had one of his many women waiting for him.

"Give me a second. Smitty told me you weren't coming until about thirty minutes from now." Shawn said as he quickly disappeared down the skinny hallway going towards the bedroom. Santana helped himself to a seat on the old raggedy sofa that rested against the wall. He grabbed the F.E.D.S. magazine from the unsteady coffee table. "Damn you could of at least cleaned the place up a little!" He yelled out. "Fucking disgusting!" Santana huffed as he stomped a roach, then stood back up.

"Stop complaining. You act like you ain't never saw a roach before," Shawn laughed handing him a book bag. He never really cared too much for Santana, in his eyes he was nothing but a soft pretty boy with a whole lot of mouth, but couldn't back it up.

"Don't get mad at me because you like living like an animal. The gorgeous gangsta ain't used to these kind of living conditions, smell me?" He said as he unzipped the book bag and peeked inside. "Beautiful" he said zipping the bag back up. "Imma scream at you later."

"A'ight young blood," Shawn said as he gave Santana a pound. Before Santana made it to the door, he heard a loud series of gunshots. He and Shawn quickly dove to the ground as bullets and broken glass came raining in. Santana quickly grabbed his .380 from his pocket and removed the safety. Shawn reached under the raggedy couch and grabbed the shotgun that rested under there. When the gun shots ended the two men heard the sounds of tires screeching. Santana quickly hopped up and ran to the window. Outside he saw all the local thugs who stood in front of the building sprawled out on the concrete. Each of their bodies was riddled with bullets.

"Fuck!" he cursed. "All those niggas in front of the building is dead."

"Fuck them. Get over here and help me get this shit out of here before Five-O get here," Shawn said in a fast high pitched voice.

Shawn and Santana quickly ran to the back room. Shawn grabbed as much product as he could and stuffed it in the duffle bag that hung around his neck. "You got the money right?"

"Yeah," Santana answered, holding up the book bag. Before the two made their exit, Shawn went over to the window to see what was going on. "Fuck! We gotta go. The cops are outside!" He growled. Once the two was out of the apartment, Shawn quickly ran in the stair case and began running up the stairs, skipping two at a time. "Come on," he yelled over his shoulder.

Santana ran up the stairs breathing like he was about to die. "I'm coming," he replied, barely able to get the words out. When the two finally made it to the roof, Shawn and Santana easily walked over to the next building. The two buildings connected at the roof. Once on the next roof, the two shared a "get away" smile as they waited for the elevator.

"Let's take the stairs," Shawn teased.

"Fuck outta here," Santana wheezed, still breathing heavily. The elevator couldn't have come at a better time.

"Whoever did this is gon have to pay just for making me have to run!" he said as they entered the elevator.

"Yeah whoever did this is definitely gonna have to pay," Shawn said as he pressed the close door and lobby button at the same time.

"Got me sweating and shit! You know I don't be playing that shit," Santana continued.

"Stop crying like a little bitch." Shawn sucked his teeth and crumbled up his face.

"Bitch my ass, I don't run track. Imma smooth, fly nigga! I ain't got time for all this madness, I leave all this running shit to ugly mufucka's like you," Santana said as the elevator stopped on the lobby floor.

"Just act normal and we'll be fine," Shawn said as he stepped off the elevator, followed by Santana. The two stepped outside and saw cops everywhere.

"Damn I ain't never seen this many cops all in one place." Shawn walked right through the cops and slid in the minivan that was parked at the end of the block.

"SNEAKY THIEF"

"Damn so you just told her not to come back up here no more?" Skip asked in disbelief.

"Yeah I had to. She's such a young girl. She could be doing so many other things. Just because my life is over doesn't mean hers has to end as well." Ali said, munching on some Doritos. He loved Nancy with all of his heart, but he just couldn't allow her to stop her life just because of his situation.

"I feel you, but have you ever thought that maybe you might be her life?" Skip pointed out.

"That might be the case but I think it's just selfish of me to have her keep coming up here knowing that I'm never coming home." Ali paused. "I'm in here for life, and I ain't never getting out...Never!"

"I feel you," Skip replied as he stood up. "Imma head to my cell real quick and write April a letter before the count." He gave Ali dap then made his exit.

When Skip made it back to his cell, something seemed out of place. He quickly looked under his bed and noticed that his pair of shell toe Adidas were no longer there. "What the fuck?" He cursed loudly, looking around his cell. Once Skip searched his entire cell, he knew he had been robbed. He quickly stormed out of his cell and made it back to Ali's cell. "Somebody went up in my cell and took my new shell toes," Skip fumed.

"Don't sweat it. Whoever we see rocking some new shell toes, we straight washing them up." (Beating them up) Ali said in a calm tone.

"I'm about to ask the cat in the cell next to mine if he saw anybody in my cell," Skip said, already heading in that direction. He walked up to the man who resided in the cell next to his with Ali on his heels. "Yo fam you seen anybody up in my cell?"

"Nah, I don't know nothing. "The man said waving his hands like he was praising Jesus as he tried to walk off.

"Get the fuck over here." Skip growled as he grabbed the man and slammed him against the wall. "Who was in my cell?"

"Hey is everything alright over here?" A big C.O. asked walking over. "Is there a problem over here Ali?"

"Nah everything's cool." Ali replied as he tapped Skip on the shoulder. "We out."

"Imma see you later," Skip told the man as him and Ali walked off.

"Don't worry, we gon make that nigga talk" Ali said as he laid down on his bed. "Go write April a letter and holla at me later." Once Skip had left, Ali stared up at the ceiling thinking about how the last eight months of his life had played out. As he laid there thinking, he realized it was so many thing he wish he could have went back and changed.

Tears of a Hustler 3

"BUSINESS IS BUSINESS"

"How did everything play out?" Pauleena asked as she watched Roy and Eraser Head enter her office, both wearing smiles on their faces.

"Piece of cake," Eraser Head said, flopping down on the couch.

"We tore that whole building up," Roy volunteered.

"I don't know why they would open up on one of our blocks and not think nothing was going to happen." Pauleena said, seeming confused. If anybody knew her or anything about her then they had to have known that there would definitely be consequences for their actions.

"They must think shit is sweet because G-Money is gone," Eraser Head said out loud.

"Well them clowns got another thing coming," Pauleena said simply. "One man doesn't run the show, and doesn't any one man stop the show either."

* * *

Shawn pulled up on the block and let the engine die. "That Moonie right there in front of the Chinese restaurant?"

"Yeah that's her," Santana confirmed as the two headed over in her direction. Moonie stood in front of the Chinese restaurant holding a conversation on her cell phone when she saw Shawn and Santana walking up.

"Yo Moonie is Smitty or Marvin around?" Shawn asked. Moonie quickly hushed him by holding up one finger. "You got until noon tomorrow to have that money!" She barked into the receiver then pressed the end button on her cell phone. "What y'all niggas want?"

"Somebody just shot up the stash crib," Shawn told her.

"Get the fuck out of here!" Moonie said in disbelief. "Which one?"

"Some things Never Change"

The barber shop was packed as usual. B.E.T. played on the television as several conversations were being held at the same time. Marvin sat in the barber chair getting a fresh cut like he did every two weeks. "Make sure you don't push my hair line back."

"It can't go back no further," Eddie joked. Eddie had been Marvin's barber since he was a kid. Not only was he his barber, but he was also Romelo's barber. The only thing was he had to make house visits whenever Romelo needed a cut. But the pay in return was well worth the travel. "How's your father?"

"Busy as usual," Marvin replied. "You know he's all work and no play."

"Yeah and I see you learned from the best." Eddie said with a raised eyebrow.

"Yo Five-O coming," a man waiting to get a haircut called out.

"What the fuck these fools want?" Eddie asked out loud as he watched to two detectives enter the shop. Detective Nelson and Detective Bradley entered the barber shop and all conversations came to an end.

"Can I help you gentlemen?" Eddie asked.

"Yeah we would just like to have a word with Marvin," Detective Nelson said politely, with a little smirk on his face.

"I'm listening," Marvin said in an uninterested tone.

"You mind stepping outside?"

"Step outside for what? Whatever you can ask me outside, you can ask me right here." Marvin said not budging.

"Listen smart ass, we know what you and your crew are up to," Detective Bradley said with a sweep of his arm. "We don't care about you selling drugs, but when people start getting murdered, our bosses start getting in our ass and when the bosses get in our asses, we get into your pockets. Comprehende?" (understand)

"Sorry detectives. I would love to help but unfortunately I have no idea what y'all are talking about." Marvin chuckled.

"Fifteen thousand a month and you won't hear from us again or any other cops," Detective Nelson threw the offer on the table. Word on the streets was Marvin and his crew was on the come up, and Detective Nelson wanted a piece of the action.

"Like I just told your partner, I don't know what you're talking about." Marvin said sticking to his story.

"Well maybe we should go have a word with your father Romelo," Detective Nelson said with a smile. From the look on Marvin's face, he knew he struck a nerve. "You got two weeks to decide what it's going to be. I just pray you make the right choice." Detective Nelson said as he and his partner filed for the exit.

"Bastards!" Eddie growled once they were gone.

"You know those detectives?" Marvin asked curiously.

"Who doesn't? That's the same detective that took Ali down and got G-Money killed," Eddie said out loud.

"Damn they must be some good detectives," Marvin said stepping out the chair.

"Good detectives, my ass! Those are two of the most crooked detectives in the whole city."

"So what do they want with me?" Marvin asked.

"What everybody wants....Money!" Eddie replied.

"They barking up the wrong tree because Marvin doesn't get extorted," he said simply. As hard as he had to work to get to where he was at, there was no way he was just going to GIVE Detective Nelson his hard earned money.

"The best thing for you to do is go holla at Romelo and see what he think is best," Eddie suggested.

"I think I might just do that," Marvin said as he paid Eddie and gave him a pound.

"Be careful" Eddie yelled out as he watched Marvin and his entourage make their exit.

"CHANGE OF PLANS"

"Where you think you going?" Monique asked with her arms folded across her chest.

"Out!" Loco replied filing for the door.

"Out where?" Monique asked standing in front of the door so Loco couldn't leave. For the past week she hadn't seen much of him, and she was tired of the bullshit.

"Come on don't start this bullshit! Can you act like you got some sense for once please?"

"Sense my ass. You still ain't tell me where you going," Monique said, snaking her neck.

"Bitch I just told you I'm going out. Now get the fuck out of my way." Loco growled as he grabbed Monique by her arms and spun her out of his way."

"Keep your fucking hands off me!" Monique yelled. "And don't even think about coming back mufucka!" She screamed slamming the door behind him.

"Crazy ass bitch," Loco mouthed as he walked down the hallway.

"I don't know why you put up with that bitch." Gunplay said holding the elevator.

"I don't know either," Loco said, stepping inside.

"You be too nice." Gunplay said, pressing the lobby button.

"Fuck all that, how we looking?" Loco said, changing the subject.

"We looking good," Gunplay said as the elevator reached the lobby. "Only problem is we running low on product. What should we do?"

"Let me worry about that. You just keep doing what you do." Loco stated. "But what's good with the homies?"

"Yeah I had Young Taz round up all the Bloods in the hood and they all behind us a hundred and ten percent," Gunplay told him.

"That's what I like to hear," Loco said as he noticed two undercover cops fastly approaching. "You clean?"

"Yeah I passed my ratchet off to Taz before I came to see you," Gunplay said.

"HANDS ON THE GATE GENTLEMEN!" one of the officers yelled, flashing his badge.

"Why, what's the problem?" Loco asked defensively.

"We ask the questions around here." The other officer cut in. He grabbed Loco and shoved him on the gate.

"Yeah, you a real tough guy, hiding behind that badge." Loco hissed as the undercover officer frisked him. The officer handcuffed Loco before he replied. "I fuck guys like you up all the time just for fun." He said as he dug in Loco's pockets and pulled out a bag of weed. "What's this?"

"Come on, y'all on some petty shit." Loco sighed. "Y'all aint got nothing better to do?"

"Why do you guys have on so much red? Are y'all Bloods?"

"Fuck all that! What's the charges?" Gunplay huffed as the other officer roughly searched his pockets. "What have we here?" He said retrieving a thick knot of cash from Gunplay's pocket.

"Black people aren't allowed to have money?" Gunplay asked as the undercover officers shoved him and Loco in the backseat of the unmarked vehicle.

"Yo what the fuck?" Taz and about ten Bloods yelled with their hands in the air.

"Fuck the police!" A kid with a red flag on his head yelled.

"These motherfuckers always doing this shit," Taz said as he fished around in the garbage can until he found an empty forty ounce bottle. Once the undercover officers got in their vehicle, Taz tossed the empty bottle. It exploded on the windshield of the car as it sped off. "Faggots!" He yelled as he and the rest of the crew watched the unmarked vehicle bend the corner.

Ten minutes after the D's left, Taz saw an all black Escalade pull up to the curb. Eraser Head stepped out of the truck followed by two soldiers. "Taz, what's good my nigga? Where's Loco?" He asked giving him dap.

"The D's just snatched him and Gunplay up."

"Why, what happened?"

"Shit, you know how them boys do. Harassing brothers for no reason" Taz told him.

"A'ight, make sure you tell Loco to come see me as soon as he gets out, you dig?"

"I got you," Taz said as he watched Eraser Head and his soldiers head back to towards the Escalade.

"YOU CAN'T BE SERIOUS"

Marvin pulled up in the driveway of his father's house and killed the engine. He slid out the BMW followed by one of his diesel enforcers. Marvin stormed in Romelo's office without knocking. "What the fuck? I've been calling you all fucking day!"

"I've been busy," Romelo said nonchalantly. "What can I do for you?"

"Yo, I was in the barbershop letting Eddie hook me up. Then these two detectives walked up in the joint talking reckless."

"What were they saying?" Romelo asked, finally giving his son his undivided attention. From the way his son was worked up he knew it had to be something important.

"Talking about, I better give them fifteen gees every month."

"For what?"

"Just cause. Then they told me I got two weeks to make a decision." Marvin told his father.

"So what you going to do?"

"I ain't paying them crackers shit." Marvin said in an even tone. "Pay them for what? Fuck outta here!"

Romelo laughed out loud before responding. "You're definitely your father's child cause I wouldn't pay them shit either. I done already greased enough palms for the both of us."

"These fucking cops are the real criminals," Marvin said as he felt his cell phone vibrating. "Yeah, what up?"

"What up? Where you at?" Smitty asked.

"I'm with the old man."

"A'ight bet. I'm right around the corner. I'll be there in a minute." Smitty said, ending the call. He needed to talk to Marvin about Pauleena and figured he should do it in person.

"Who you calling an old man?" Romelo smiled once Marvin got off the phone. "I might be old but I can still get in where I fit in."

"I hear you talking," Marvin said waving him off. He was still pissed at how the detective had come at him.

"Your birthday is in two weeks. What you got planned?" Tango asked reminding everybody he was in the room.

"Not sure yet," Marvin shrugged. "I think Smitty might be planning this big party for me but he think I don't know."

"Speak of the devil," Romelo said as he saw Smitty and Moonie pull up on his surveillance monitor. "Tango let those two loose cannons in."

"We got problems," Smitty said as soon as he walked in the office with Moonie close on his heels.

"Talk to me," Marvin said turning to face Smitty.

"This bitch retaliated. Tore up the whole block!"

"Who, Pauleena?"

Smitty nodded his head yes. "What you wanna do?"

"You need to let me smoke that bitch already." Moonie blurted out.

"In due time, first things first, let's just keep on taking over as many blocks as possible. Trust me, Pauleena won't last very long. Let's just stick to the plan," Marvin instructed. He knew Moonie, and Smitty were dying to put in work. He figured the longer he kept them on the leash, when he took them off it would be hard to stop them. Marvin didn't want to just rush into things with Pauleena especially since he didn't know too much about her. He'd just heard a few stories here and there.

"I told you Pauleena wasn't going to be a pushover." Romelo said.

"She can get it just like anybody else," Moonie said in a stern voice.

"I never said she couldn't. But I think it would have been smart if the two of you would have worked together." Romelo said. "It's more than enough money for both of y'all to eat.

"Fuck working together. If you want the crown you gotta go out and take it," Marvin said pouring himself a drink. "Plus I ain't comfortable with a female wearing the crown."

"Me either," Tango agreed from the side line. "That's why I never wanted to be the boss. Too many tough decisions to be made."

"Being the boss must run in our blood." Marvin muttered.

"It sure does son." Romelo said proudly. "Listen, I gotta get ready to go take care of some business but, if that detective guy keeps fucking with you let me know and I'll take care of it for you."

"I ain't worried about that clown." Marvin said waving off that last comment.

Tears of a Hustler 3

"I DON'T THINK SO"

"Good looking papi," Loco said as he gave the cab driver a twenty dollar bill and slid out the backseat. As he headed towards his building, he saw Taz, Gunplay, and the rest of the crew posted up.

"What's good my nigga? When you get out?" Loco asked giving Gunplay a pound.

"Like forty five minutes ago," Gunplay replied. "Fucking crackers, wasting my fucking time!"

"Yo right after the D's picked y'all up, Eraser Head came through looking for you." Taz said.

"Word? What he talking about?" Loco asked curiously.

"Nothing, he just said for you to call him when you get out."

"He wants that bread?" Gunplay said out loud.

"Fuck him," Loco grumbled as his cell phone started ringing. He noticed it was a blocked number. "Hello?" He answered.

"What's really good?" The voice on the other end said.

"Who this?"

"Ali."

"Oh shit! My nigga, what's good?"

"Ain't shit. Hold on for a second. Yo, Mya put the phone down, so I can holla at my man real quick," he told the girl who was doing the three way call for him.

"Ok Baby," she said.

"Yeah so how it's looking out there?" Ali asked.

"It's looking lovely out here but I needed to holla at you on the serious tip."

"I'm listening."

"It's like his. I'm dealing with his cat named Eraser Head, but the only reason I was fucking with him was cause of G-Money. But now since G-Money ain't here no more I don't see the point."

"I feel you," Ali paused. "So what you tryna do, your own thing?"

"Yeah I'm trying to pick up where you left off. You know, help the community out. Give people jobs and shit like that, smell me?"

"I can dig it. But imma let you know it's harder than it looks." Ali told him.

"Yeah I know. B ut it's fucked up out here with this recession going on and all that. All these young niggas out here sticking up anything moving," Loco said scornfully.

"I be knowing, but you know Eraser Head and Pauleena ain't gon be too happy to hear that," Ali pointed out.

"Fuck them! If they got a problem, they can come see me."

"They will," Ali assured him.

"I'll make sure I'll be real right when they do. Oh yeah, what you want me to do with your cut of the money?"

"You can just give it to Nancy."

"Who, you talking about, the shorty who was holding you down while we was up top? Loco asked.

"Yeah."

"She still standing strong?"

"Yeah, but I had to let her go," Ali told him.

"Why, she was fucking around on you?"

"Nah I just didn't want her wasting her time anymore. She mad young. She can be doing so many other things with her life, feel me? I just felt like I was being selfish by letter her continue to come and see me, you dig?"

"I feel where you coming from."

"But listen brother, this phone is about to cut off so imma scream at you another time. Be careful out there."

When Loco got off the phone Gunplay noticed how serious his friend's face looked. "Everything a'ight?"

"That was my man Ali. Fuck Eraser Head! We doing our own thing, he announced.

"That's what I'm talking about," Gunplay said splitting open a Dutch and dumping the guts on the ground. "But what we gon do about a connect?"

"Imma swing uptown and holla at one of my niggas I used to deal with back in the day," Loco said. "The rest of y'all be ready just in case Eraser Head come through on some other shit."

"That boy ain't stupid. He can come around here acting stupid if he wants to." Taz said as he spit on the ground.

"I'm about to head upstairs and make a few calls to see if I can get my hands on some butter," Loco said as he gave the men dap then headed inside the building.

* * *

Silk White

"BETTER DAYS"

"Why you always got a mean look on your face?" Smitty asked taking his eyes off the road so he could glance at Moonie.

"Because, I don't like that bitch, Pauleena! Bitch, need to be taught a lesson!" Moonie huffed.

"In due time."

"Due time my ass, I'm tired of waiting." Moonie continued to rant.

"Well you won't have to wait much longer. Marvin already gave us the green light, so you already know what time it is," Smitty said as he pulled over and double parked in front of the building he was looking for.

"Who we hitting?" Moonie asked, slipping her hands into a pair of leather gloves.

"Some cat named Mike," Smitty answered quickly.

"Mike?" Moonie said with a confused look on her face. "Who, the fuck is that?"

"Marvin said he gotta go so he gotta go," Smitty shrugged his shoulders as him and Moonie slid out of the Buick. Once inside the building, Smitty and Moonie jogged up the steps until they reached the third floor. Before the two exited the staircase, they made sure to slide their ski masks on to hide their identity.

"Let's keep this shit short and sweet," Smitty said, screwing the silencer on his Beretta as the two made their way to the door they were looking for. On a silent count of three Smitty turned and shot the lock off the door. Moonie rushed inside the apartment first. She spotted a woman in the kitchen standing over the stove. Moonie aimed her 9mm at the woman's leg and pulled the trigger. When the shot went off Mike quickly appeared from out the back room with a nervous and scared look on his face.

Smitty quickly entered the apartment and put a bullet in each one of Mike's legs dropping him right where he stood.

"Argggggg!"   Mike screamed as he clutched both of his legs.

"Where's the money?"   Smitty asked calmly standing over the wounded man.   Word on the streets was Mike was in charge of collecting all of Pauleena's drug money before turning it in to Eraser Head.

"Ain't no money here" Mike smiled. "And even if it was I still wouldn't give it to you" he laughed loudly laying in a pool of his own blood.

"Don't be a hero, just give us Pauleena's money and we'll let you live." Smitty lied his main concern was collecting the money.

"Fuck you, i'll rather deal with you two dummies before I cross Pauleena" Mike said.

"So you willing to lose your own life to protect this bitch!?" Moony snapped as she knelt down and began pistol whipping Mike. She mashed his face in until her arm got tired. "Mufucka!" She growled placing the barrel of her gun to his temple and pulled the trigger. Moonie then made her way into the kitchen, and filled Mike's girlfriend body with bullets.

"Damn" Smitty huffed once the two got back in the car. "Think you can save some action for me next time?"

"Sorry" Moonie apologized. "But I'm just so sick and tired of hearing about this bitch, I'm sick of her."

"You just an action freak" Smitty said as he weaved in and out of traffic. "But what's your big beef with Pauleena?"

"I hate bitches like her" Moonie said. "Everything I got I had to work for, and I can't stand bitches that who gets everything handed to them, I call'em spoon fed bitches, and it's always the fake bitches who get the shit handed to them."

"From the stories I've heard, Pauleena ain't no pushover, or weak type of bitch" Smitty reminded Moonie.

Moonie sucked her teeth. "Whatever."

Minutes later Smitty pulled up in front of Moonie's. "I'll be by to scoop you up tomorrow" he said as he watched her head inside.

Moonie stepped foot in her crib, and immediately ran some water to fill up her hot tub. On the outside she seemed as tough as nails, but on the inside she was still a woman. She kicked off her Ugg boots, removed her clothes, grabbed herself a glass of wine and hopped in her hot tub. No matter how her day went the hot tub always seemed to make Moonie feel better. Moonie soaked in her tub, sipping on her wine thinking about Pauleena. The real reason she disliked the woman so much was because Pauleena was in the position that she wanted to be in, and in her heart Moonie felt that Pauleena didn't put in enough work to have that spot. Moonie's ringing phone snapped her out of her thoughts. "Yo what up?" She answered.

"Yo what up, this Santana."

"What do you want?" Moonie asked in mid-sip.

"I got some bread for Marvin, and Smitty said to call you and leave it with you, I'm about three minutes away from your crib, I can easily just drop that off real quick" Santana suggested.

"A'ight hurry up" Moonie said ending the call. She finished up her glass of wine, and quickly poured herself another glass. Seconds later

Moonie heard a loud knock at her door. "Mufucka said three minutes" Moonie huffed as she hopped out the hot tub, threw on her robe then headed to the door. She snatched the door open and saw Santana standing on the other side. "Fuck you knocking on my door like you the police for?"

"My bad" Santana apologized. "But I gotta pee real badly. Can I please use your bathroom?"

"Hurry up" Moonie said as she took the book bag from his hands, and then stepped to the side so he could enter. She poured herself another glass of wine as she peeked inside the book bag.

"Damn is it necessary for you to have this many guns lying around?" Santana said appearing out of nowhere.

"In my line of work a gun is my best friend" Moonie sipped from her glass.

"Damn I ain't know you was working with all that?" Santana said looking at Moonie's nice shape through her robe how the robe clung to her body he could tell that she was naked underneath. "I can do a few things with a body like that?"

Moonie laughed. "Nigga please, you can't do shit, you used to fucking with them young bitches"

"You bugging" he said pouring himself a glass of wine.

"Yo what you think you doing?" Moonie asked looking at him like he was crazy.

"I'm having a drink with you" Santana said as he pulled at the string on her robe causing the front of the robe to open up. Moonie thought about stopping him, but decided to see what Santana was about. Besides she'd been so busy with work that she had to put sex on the back burner.

"Don't start nothing you can't finish" Moonie said in a sexually charged voice as she watch Santana play with her clitoris piercing with his finger.

"Oh trust and believe I finish everything I start" Santana assured Moonie as he lifted her up on top of the counter and watched as she spread her legs apart.

"Come taste this pussy!" Moonie demanded. She closed her eyes and bit down on her bottom lip as she felt Santana's tongue lick, and massage her sensitive spot. Santana kissed, sucked, and licked all over Moonie's pussy, the louder she moaned it turned him on, and the better he performed. Moonie wrapped her legs around the back of Santana's neck, and clawed at the top of her head, as she felt herself releasing in his mouth. Once Santana was done he lifted Moonie up off the counter and carried her over to the couch, where he slipped a condom on and penetrated her from behind.

"Ahh" Moonie moaned as Santana slid in and out of her walls. Once Santana had worked his way in, he began to speed up his strokes. Moonie squeezed on a pillow and took the dick like a big girl.

Once the two were done Santana laid back on the couch with a smile on his face. He liked Moonie, but just felt she was just a little too rough around the edges, but with his help he felt he might could change that.

"Fuck you over there smiling for?" Moonie said snapping Santana out of his thoughts. "And you look a little too comfortable, get Yo shit and get the fuck out!"

"Ma calm down" Santana stood to his feet still naked. "I got a few things I need to take care of, but I'll definitely love to see you again" he licked his lips.

"Nigga please" Moonie said as she covered herself back up with her robe. "You ain't never getting no more this good pussy and you better not leave my crib and start running your mouth."

"I look like one of these clowns you used to fucking with?" Santana asked as he moved in close and kissed her neck. "I would like to do this again soon."

"Back up a taste" Moonie pushed Santana back. "It's time for you to leave."

Santana smiled as he quickly got dressed, and left. Moonie locked the door behind him, and then made her way to the bedroom. Inside Moonie kind of liked Santana, but his childish ways, and handsome features is what scared her, she didn't have time for games, and needed to stay focused with the mission at hand.

***

"Out Of Luck"

Four all black Denali SUVs pulled up back to back in front of the projects. Pauleena sat in the third SUV with her legs crossed sipping on a glass of wine. Today was a day in her life that she would never forget. "You sure this where this cat lives?"

"Yes I got a man in the staircase right now who's been watching Carl's crib all day" Eraser Head told her.

Pauleena sighed loudly. "Let's go get this shit over with." Her big Muslim body guard Malcolm quickly hopped out of the driver's seat, and walked to the back door, and opened it for his boss. Pauleena stepped out looking like a million bucks followed by Eraser Head. Seven black Muslims all wearing black suits hopped out of the SUVs and escorted Pauleena in the building, and up to Carl's floor. Eraser Head and Malcolm kicked open Carl's front door, then quickly barged inside.

Carl sat in his couch watching TV when his front door came crashing open, followed by men busting inside with guns pointed in his face. "What's all this about?" Carl asked with a confused look on his face.

"You know exactly what this is about" Pauleena said entering the apartment. From the look on Carl's face she could tell that he didn't know who she was, but he was definitely about to find out. "Did you kill G-Money?"

"Yes I did" Carl said confidently. "He disrespected, and violated me in front of my son, and for that he had to pay."

Pauleena smiled. "And now you have to pay" she said as she pulled a .380 from the small of her back. Just as she was about to pull the trigger, little Bobby came running out the back room. "No please don't hurt my daddy" he cried as he hugged his father.

"You kill me in front of my son?" Carl asked looking Pauleena dead in her eyes. He didn't fear no man or woman, but if it was his time to go he didn't want it to be in front of his son.

Pauleena looked down at Carl with a straight face, and pulled the trigger blowing his brains out right in front of little Bobby. She then trained her gun on the young boy, and sent bullets into the boy's boney chest killing him instantly. "A body for a body" she said as she turned, handed her gun to Malcolm then made her exit.

Back in the Denali everyone was quiet, they knew Pauleena had just crossed the line, but they knew she had to do what she had to do. If the streets spotted any signs of weakness, every stick up kid in the world would be looking for her, and hustlers would be looking to take her spot. Pauleena was on top, and she planned on doing whatever needed to be done to stay on top.

"I heard Marvin is supposed to be having a birthday party next week" Eraser Head said breaking the silence.

"Word where at?" Pauleena asked helping herself to another glass of wine.

"Some club downtown."

"Keep me posted" Pauleena said with a smile. "I wouldn't miss that party for the world."

"It's Lonely At The Top"

Nancy sat in the hot tub in deep thought, she still couldn't believe that Ali had refused to see her, and had officially broken up with her. Never in a million years would she think Ali would ever stop speaking to her. He told her he was only doing it, because he didn't want Nancy to suffer, but what he realized was that the longer Nancy went without seeing him, the more she would suffer.

Tears fell from Nancy's eyes the more she thought about Ali. She had written him plenty of letters since their last visit, but still he wouldn't reply. Coco was babysitting Little Ali for the weekend hoping Nancy would use this time to get herself together, and hopefully find herself a new man, but it was no use, Ali held the key to Nancy's heart.

Once Nancy got out of the hot tub, she got dressed and decided to treat herself to a nice dinner at one of her favorite Japanese restaurants. Nancy threw on one her nice grey business suites, some grey matching pumps, and headed out the door.

* * *

Marvin sat in the passenger seat of Smitty's Range Rover, sipping on a cup of vodka. His birthday party was only a few days away, and he still didn't know what he was going to do about Detective Nelson. He knew anyway he looked at it; it was going to be a problem an ugly problem.

"Any suggestions on what we should do about this punk ass cop?" Smitty asked sitting behind the wheel.

"Not yet" Marvin replied. "I'm still thinking about how I should play it."

"If we pay this cock sucker we'll be paying him forever" Smitty pointed out. "But if we don't then, he's going to keep the heat on us so either way you look at it we're fucked. You saw what happened to G-Money, and Ali."

"Fuck that cause I ain't Ali, and you damn sure ain't G-Money" Marvin chuckled. "Fuck this cracker, I ain't paying him shit!"

"Whatever you wanna do, I'm down," Smitty said stopping for a red light. As Marvin looked out the window he saw the same chick who's car he bumped into a few weeks ago sitting by the window eating alone. "Yo pull over real quick" he said. He didn't plan on letting the woman out of his site this time. When Marvin wanted something he'd never stop until his mission was accomplished. "Yo I'll be right back, imma run in there real quick, and holla at shorty."

"You want me to roll with you?" Smitty asked.

"Nah I'm good" Marvin said lifting up his shirt flashing the butt of his .45 as he hopped out the whip, and headed inside the Japanese restaurant.

Nancy sat her table enjoying her meal, when Marvin came and sat directly across from her in the booth.

"Hey baby wassup" he said flashing his million dollar smile. "Why, you ain't never call me," he asked as he flagged down the waitress and ordered another bottle of wine.

"Ummm do I know you?" Nancy asked with a slight attitude. She knew exactly who he was, but she didn't like how he had just helped himself to a seat.

"You don't remember me?" Marvin asked with a smile. He knew she was bullshitting, but decided to play along. "I couldn't wait to run into you again" he said as he grabbed Nancy's hand and caressed it.

"Why?" Nancy asked removing her hand from his grip.

"Because I want to make you mine, and treat you like a queen."

"Why?" Nancy replied. "You don't even know me or nothing about me."

"I want to get to know you" Marvin said smoothly as the waiter brought over the bottle of wine he ordered. "Give me a chance to show you what I'm about."

"Sorry, but I already have a man" Nancy said sipping from her glass. "And I don't think he would approve of me getting to know you better."

"If you have a man, then why does he have you sitting in this restaurant all alone?" Marvin asked. Just from hearing her say that, he knew either two things. Either she had some nigga that either treated her like shit, and she was eating alone because he didn't have time for her, or either her man was in jail.

"I have my reasons" Nancy shot back not wanting to reveal too much information. She couldn't front, Marvin was very handsome, but she refused to talk to him thinking it would be disrespectful to Ali.

"I don't know what's going on with you, and your man, and I don't care but what I do know is that a beautiful woman like yourself should never have to eat alone" Marvin said in a matter of fact tone.

"So what's your story?" Nancy said quickly changing the subject. "Where is your girl?"

"Girl?" Marvin repeated. "I only deal with women, and right now I haven't found that right one" he said looking in Nancy's eyes. He could tell just by looking at her that she hadn't been fucked real good in a while, and if he got the chance he planned on doing just that.

"I hear that" Nancy smiled as she finished up her glass of wine. "It was nice wrapping with you, but it's getting late, and I should be going" she said pulling out her debit card.

"Don't insult me like that" Marvin huffed as he reached down into his pocket and pulled out three fifty dollar bills and sat them on the table.

"Thank you" Nancy said as she got up and exited the restaurant. Just as she made it to her car Marvin stopped her.

"Can I get your phone number before you go?"

"No" Nancy replied quickly. "Didn't I tell you I had a man?"

"I heard you, but I think I can treat you better then he can if you give me the chance" Marvin said. Nancy didn't reply she just smiled as she got inside her car. "Thank you, but no thank you."

"I'm having a party for my birthday next week, I would love it if you, and you man showed up, I would love to see who this lucky man is" Marvin said as he handed her a flyer to the party. "This going to be the biggest party in town, and I would love for you to be here."

"I'll think about it" Nancy said as she closed her door, and pulled off leaving Marvin standing there. Marvin stood there until Nancy's headlights disappeared. He didn't know how he was going to get her, but one thing he knew was he wasn't going to stop until he had her. As Marvin stood there his cell phone rung, he looked down at his iPhone and saw Moonie's name flashing across the screen. "Yo what up?" he answered.

"Where you at nigga?" Moonie asked.

"Down by that new Japanese restaurant downtown."

"I'm like five minutes away, imma swing through and scoop you up," Moonie said ending the call. Ten minutes later Marvin saw Moonie's all black Lexus coupe pull up to the curb.

"What you down this way?" Moonie asked pulling back out into traffic.

"Trying scoop this chick" Marvin answered.

"That's not like you to be chasing a bitch" Moonie pointed out. "She must be a fly ass bitch."

"I can't even front" Marvin said keeping it real. "I really like shorty, I gotta make her mine."

"What!?" Moonie said looking over at Marvin like he was crazy. Ever since she met Marvin she had never heard him talk about a woman like this. Instantly she figured who ever this woman was would be no good for him. "We need to get a drink so you can tell me all about this chick" she said parking her Lexus a block away from the lounge.

Marvin and Moonie stepped foot in the lounge and saw that the spot was packed. "Damn" Moonie said as the two squeezed their way over to the bar. "Yo lemme get a bottle of Ciroc!" She yelled over the music as she and Marvin scanned over the crowd.

* * *

Over on the other side of the lounge sat Roy, Eraser Head, and three other goons. "I'm tired of playing with these niggaz!" Roy said in a drunken slur. He wasn't pissy drunk yet, but he wasn't far from there either. "I wish Pauleena would give us the green light so we can tear shit up already!"

"She knows what she doing" Eraser Head said pouring himself another drink. "Be patient"

"Nah I put in work for a living, that's what I do" Roy bragged. "I'm tired of waiting, we in New York, and all these niggaz see me and Pauleena as is country niggaz, but I got something for these mufucka's."

"What you got for em?" Eraser Head asked. He was just making conversation. He knew Roy was just talking because he was drunk.

"Some hot ones" Roy said as he looked up and saw Marvin and Moonie standing over by the bar.

"Fuck these niggaz doing up in here?" He said out loud as he headed over towards the bar area with his three goons in tow. When Eraser Head looked up and saw where Roy was headed, immediately he knew some shit was about to go down. "Shit!" He cursed as he followed Roy and the goons over towards the bar. He hadn't spoken to Pauleena so he wasn't sure if she wanted them to make a move like this, but now it was too late.

Marvin stood over by the bar sipping on his drink when he notice some drunk looking nigga step to him.

"Yo fam!" Roy said with a grin on his face. "Keep Yo mufucking peoples out of Pauleena's territory or else we going to have problems understand?"

"Fuck is you, her message boy?" Moonie butted in from the sideline.

"Bitch! I wasn't talking to you!" Roy barked talking to Moonie, but his eyes remained on Marvin. "So I suggest you back the fuck up, before you get smacked the fuck up!"

"What!?" Moonie said with her face crumbled up, as she cleared her throat, and hog spit in Roy's face. Before Roy got a chance to respond, Marvin had already busted the Ciroc bottle over his head knocking him out cold. Eraser Head quickly retaliated with a right hook to the side of Marvin's head, from there an all out brawl broke out.

Moonie jumped into the brawl, and did the best she could to hold Marvin down, until a few bouncers came and separated the two crews and tossed them out the lounge.

Roy wanted to keep the fight going, but the police who stood outside the club kept the two crews separated with treats of taking everyone to jail.

"Don't worry imma see you again" Roy said with a grin on his face as he and Marvin eye boxed all the way to their cars. Both men knew the next time they crossed one another's path some blood was going to be spilled.

* * *

"The Tough Guy"

Ali sat in his cell looking at a picture of Nancy, and Lil Ali. He felt bad for telling Nancy not to come see him anymore, but he felt like that would be best for everyone. He couldn't stand to see Nancy crying when their visits were over every time it was time for her to leave. All Ali wanted was for her to be was stress free. If he allowed her to continue to visit him he felt he would only be bringing her down. Just because his life was over didn't mean hers had to end as well.

"I love y'all" Ali whispered to the picture as he stuck it back inside of his bible as he heard his cell door crack open.

Crystal stepped in Ali's cell with a smile on her face. "Hey Ali, wassup?"

"Chilling" Ali replied with a smile on his face. It had been a while since he and Crystal had sex, and right now that was just what he needed. "What brings you down this way?" He asked sitting up on his bunk.

"You have a new cellmate" Crystal said nodding towards the big solid light skin brother that stood next to her. "Hey I don't want no trouble out of you!" She said sternly to the big man.

The Big man sucked his teeth. "Fuck is you talking about?" He huffed. "Just stay the fuck out my way" he scoffed as he made his way inside the cell.

"You be careful" Crystal mouthed to Ali as she turned and went on about her business.

"What's ya name fam?" Ali asked getting up off of his bed.

"Big Blood" the big man answered sizing Ali up. Big Blood was known in the streets for his ruthlessness, and his gang affiliation. He was a legend in the streets, and his name was well known on Rikers Island.

"I'm Ali" he said matching Big Blood's stare. "You got the top bunk, we have to live together so let's just make the best out of this."

"Nah nigga you got me fucked up!" Big Blood said removing his shirt showing off his body full of tattoos. "Big Blood don't do the top bunk, I need that bottom joint" he said snatching Ali's sheets, and pillow off the bed onto the floor.

Ali looked at his pillow and sheets on the floor, then quickly turned and punched Big Blood in his face. The punch had no effect on Big Blood as he grabbed Ali in a bear hug, and belly to belly slammed him on the floor. Once he was on top of Ali he began punching wildly hitting Ali where ever he could.

Skip sat rested in his cell three cells down from Ali's when he heard a loud commotion, and hopped up to see what was going on. Skip made his way over to Ali's cell and saw some big nigga on top of Ali. Skip quickly rushed inside the cell, and snuffed Big Blood. Once Ali got up off the floor, he and Skip did their best to fuck Big Blood up. Big Blood fought both men at the same time, and dished out just as much as he took. Minutes later Crystal and three other C.O.'s bum rushed the cell, and separated the three men.

"Imma see you again fam!" Big Blood yelled as the police roughly escorted him out of the cell.

"Y'all alright?" Crystal asked noticing that Ali had a bloody nose, and Skip had a busted lip. "Y'all need to go to the nurse?"

"Nah we good" Ali replied as he gave Skip a pound. "Good looking."

"Who, the fuck was that nigga?" Skip asked.

"Some clown named Big Blood" Ali answered as he grabbed a towel and cleaned his nose. He didn't know what the big man's problem was, but one thing he did know was that he would definitely being seeing Big Blood again.

* * *

Coco sat at the bar area in Nancy's house helping herself to a drink while Nancy stood over the stove frying some chicken wings. She knew if her best friend stayed in the house any longer that she would eventually go crazy. She didn't know how, but she had to get Nancy out the house. "So what's up we partying tonight?"

"Partying?" Nancy yelled over her shoulder. "Yeah I'm partying right here in this house."

"Come on Nancy how long you gon stay cooped up in this house waiting for Ali to call?" Coco asked. "I like Ali, and all that but fuck him, he shitted on you so that's his loss. You are a good girl, and can get any man you damn well please."

"I don't want any man, I want Ali" Nancy said. No matter how hard she tried not to think about Ali she couldn't help it. It was like something in her brain wouldn't let her not think about him or what he was doing all day every day. "Ali is just going through something right now, and he just needs a little space" she kept telling herself.

Coco shook her head. "He told you to go enjoy your life, so why aren't you doing that?"

"I can't be out here having fun, and living it up while my man is in jail." Nancy said pouring herself a glass of wine. "I just don't feel like that's right."

"That mufucka got life Nancy, not five years, not Ten years....LIFE!" Coco pointed out. "You better wake up and smell the coffee."

"I hear you" Nancy said knowing Coco would never shut up if she didn't agree with her.

"Great" Coco said hugging her best friend. "It's not healthy to be up in this house like this all day, now go get dress we got a party to go to."

"Party?" Nancy echoed. "What party?"

"The biggest party of the year" Coco said looking at Nancy like she was crazy. "Some new guy that's been on the come up named Marvin is throwing his birthday party tonight and WE have to be there."

"What do you mean we?" Nancy laughed.

"We have to be there. Everybody and they momma gon be there, and yes you coming too, even if I have to drag you out of this house" Coco told her.

"Me and Marvin had dinner the other night" Nancy suddenly remembered. "And he did ask me to come to his party but I wasn't gon go."

"What you had dinner with Marvin, and didn't tell me?" Coco with her hands on her hip.

"I was at a restaurant having dinner, and he came inside and sat at my table" Nancy said like it was nothing. "We talked for a little while, then I left and went home."

Coco shook her head at her best friend. She couldn't understand how she always seemed to let perfect opportunities slip right through her hands.

"So you had dinner with him, and then just went home?"

"He had dinner with me" Nancy corrected her. "Then he invited me to his party."

"Well go get dressed we going to this party, Lil Ali is at my mom's house so he straight" Coco said heading towards the door. "I'll be back in two hours to pick you up" she said closing the door behind her before Nancy got a chance to protest.

"You The Man"

Romelo's limo pulled up to the back of the club, and just sat there while he poured himself a drink. "Let me holla at you for a minute before you head inside this club, and enjoy your birthday party" Romelo said looking over at Marvin.

"What's on ya mind pops?" Marvin asked as he loaded his P89 and stuck it down in his waistband. He could tell his father had a lot on his mind, and just wished he would just spit it out.

"I see you are starting to expand in this game" Romelo said with a smile. "That's a good thing, but I'm still your father, and you are my son, and my job is to always make sure you are okay."

"Spit it out pops" Marvin huffed. "Just say what you gotta say."

"I think you getting too deep into this game" Romelo told him. "I'm not telling you what do, but I do want you to make sure this is really what you want to do, before there's no way out."

"You think I can't handle it or something?" Marvin asked feeling slightly offended.

"I never said that" Romelo said. "All I'm saying is, you got enough money, think about your future, and don't put all your eggs in one basket, learn from my mistakes."

"I know what I'm doing" Marvin said not feeling how his pops was nicely trying to say he wasn't built for this lifestyle. Little did Romelo know, but Marvin was more then willing to kill and die for his empire.

"I don't want you to take what I'm saying the wrong way" Romelo said.

"I hear you" Marvin said as he slid out the back of the limo, and headed inside the club leaving his father alone.

Marvin stepped foot in the club, and immediately forgot all about what his father was talking about. He had important things on his mind. He squeezed and snaked his way through the club, speaking to all the local hustlers, and local celebrities that he knew, until he spotted Moonie and Smitty standing behind the velvet rope in a closed off V.I.P section of the club.

"Happy birthday, my nigga!" Smitty yelled as he hugged Marvin tightly. "Wanna see what I got you for bday?" Smitty asked with a smile as he escorted Marvin over to where the couches were. On the couch sat two gorgeous woman who were dressed half naked and paid for, for the night.

"That's you right there fam!" Smitty smiled as he patted his boss on the back. "Enjoy!"

"Good looking my nigga" Marvin said as he sat in between the two beautiful women.

"This is your night, tonight enjoy it" Moonie said as she handed Marvin a bottle of Coconut Ciroc. Marvin took the bottle, then reached for a glass.

"Fuck outta here!" Moonie yelled over the music removing all the glasses, and wine flutes away from Marvin's reach. "Better take that shit to the head!"

Marvin just sat back and smiled at how much love his team had for him. He knew for a fact that they would die for him if they had to. The one thing in this game that Marvin couldn't buy was loyalty. As Marvin sat back getting treated like a king buy the two women he sat in between like a sandwich, he saw his father enter the club. He still didn't like how his pops was trying to shit on his hustling skills. Later on he planned on stepping to his father, and let him know how he really felt, but now wasn't the time. Tonight was all about celebrating.

Moonie stood bobbing her head to the new Rick Ross song that blasted through the speakers. "This my shit!" She said looking over the crowd on the dance floor. As she scanned the crowd she spotted Santana over by the bar all up in some Spanish looking chick's face. Ever since the two had sex that night, she hadn't heard from Santana. "This nigga must of fell and bumped his head" Moonie said as she headed over towards the bar.

"You live around here?" Santana asked licking his lips. He'd had his eye on the Spanish chick for a while, and tonight he was making his move.

"Nah I live in Brooklyn" the Spanish chick replied.

"Oh word?" Santana smiled. "That's my second home, I stay in BK."

"Well maybe you should come see me some times" the Spanish chick said making it obvious that she was feeling Santana. She had heard that he and his crew was heavy in the streets so there was no way she was going to let him slip through her hands. "What you doing when you leave here?"

"I don't know. Why wassup?" Santana said refilling both of their flutes with straight Henny. "What you tryna do?"

"Me and a few of my home girls gon go get something to eat, I think you should join us it'll be fun" the Spanish chick smiled. Before Santana got a chance to replied Moonie stepped in between the two. "Something funny over here?" She asked looking at Santana. "Who's your little friend?" Moonie spat turning to face the Spanish chick.

"Monica" the Spanish chick said with much attitude. "Who, the fuck are you?"

"I'm the queen, you better ask about me!" Moonie said in a matter of fact tone.

"Hmmph!" Monica snickered looking Moonie up and down. "You don't look like no queen to me."

Moonie quickly turned and smacked the shit out of Monica causing people, who stood close by to back up out of the way. Santana quickly stepped in between the two women and held Monica back. "Be the bigger person" he said trying to calm her down.

"Yo let me go right now!" Monica said trying her hardest to break free. "You just gon let this raggedy bitch smack me? Nah, nah it ain't going down like that" she yelled over the loud music.

"It's not that serious ma, just chill before the bouncers toss you up outta here" Santana tried to reason with her, but from the look in Monica's eyes he knew it was no way she was going to let it go.

"Nigga you got me fucked up!" Monica yelled as three of her home girls made their way to the scene speaking in Spanish trying to figure out what was going on. "You know what?" Monica smiled as she pushed Santana off of her. "I got something for you, since you wanna be protecting bitches my brother is up in here somewhere, and I won't even be able to recognize you when they get done with you" she smiled as she walked away.

"Don't be stupid" Santana warned as he watched Monica and her home girls disappear through the crowd. He shook his head as he turned and faced Moonie. "Fuck was that all about?"

"You grinning all up in that whack bitch face, but you can't return my calls?" She said with one hand on her hip. "Have enough respect for me to at least tell a bitch something" she huffed. "That's why I don't fuck you young niggaz, y'all all a bunch of clowns."

"Clowns?" Santana echoed. "What are you talking about? First of all I thought since you looked at me like a young cat, that you wasn't really tryna be with me like that, so I was still doing me."

"Doing you?" Moonie laughed. "What you think I just give my pussy away to any nigga? I may be a little hard on the outside, but inside I'm still a woman, and you will treat me like the queen that I am."

"My bad baby" Santana said in his best pimp voice as he pulled Moonie in for a hug, and kissed her on the lips. "Don't be like that baby. We just had a little miscommunication, and I apologize."

Moonie smiled. "Got me in here ready to kill a bitch for nothing" just as the two was about to head back over to the V.I.P section, Santana heard a woman's voice yell. "YEAH THAT'S HIM RIGHT THERE!!" When Santana turned around he saw Monica pointing him out out to some short stocky Spanish man. Santana sighed loudly as he and the Spanish man walked straight up to each other and started swinging wildly, each man trying to knock the other out. Moonie quickly slipped out of her heels, and started beating the Spanish man over the head with her heel like it was a hammer, until the man's head started bleeding. Moonie kept hitting the man until she felt someone pulling on her weave from behind.

Monica pulled Moonie up off of her brother by her weave, and flung her down to the floor. When Moonie looked up she saw Smitty standing behind Monica she immediately shut her eyes as Smitty busted a bottle over Monica's head so she wouldn't get any glass in her eyes. Moonie quickly hopped up off the floor and stomped Monica out barefoot, while she watched the rest of Marvin's goons wild out on the Spanish man, and Monica home girls.

"Baby that's enough!" Santana yelled as he pulled Moonie up off of Monica, and dragged her back to the V.I.P section.

"Damn we just got here, and y'all already trying to fuck up my party," Marvin laughed. "Everybody have a drink and relax, we here to have a good time."

"What was shit about back there?" Smitty asked looking at Moonie for an answer.

"Nothing" Moonie said nonchalantly. "Some bum bitch just running off at the mouth" she didn't want everybody all up in her business, so decided to keep her and Santana's relationship a secret. Santana flopped down on the couch and helped himself to a drink. Moonie was cool, but in his eyes she wasn't wifey material, he still wanted to see other women, but he knew if he did that would fuck up his money, and that was something he couldn't risk at the moment.

"You a'ight?" Moonie asked sitting down next to Santana.

"Yeah I'm good" he replied dryly.

"I don't want no bitches all up in ya face" Moonie said sipping from her wine glass.

"Sorry about that" Santana said as he got up and walked over to where Marvin and Smitty stood. He needed to get away from Moonie for a second.

Marvin stood in the V.I.P section listening to what Smitty was saying, but he kept his eyes on his father watching his every move. He watched as Romelo strolled through the club mingling and smooth talking to the guest. Something about what his father had said to him in the car didn't sit right with him. Marvin took another swig from his bottle as he noticed Pauleena make her entrance in the club surrounded by six of her Muslim body guards. A smirk appeared on his face as he tapped Smitty. "Look who just arrived."

Once Smitty realized who he was talking about, he quickly pull his .45 from the small of his back.

"Chill!" Marvin said with a smile as he grabbed Smitty's hand. "It's my birthday and I want to enjoy it. We not pulling no hammers out unless mufucka's start acting stupid up in here."

"She must be here for a reason" Smitty pointed out.

"I know" Marvin replied taking another swig from his bottle.

Pauleena stepped in the club like she was the president. Her Muslim security cleared a path for to walk through, and made sure no one laid a finger on her. Her main purpose of coming to the club was to see what was up, in the streets. She had been hearing a lot of shit about Marvin, and his crew supposed to be taking over shit, now that she was there she wanted to hear it from Marvin's mouth herself. Malcolm led Pauleena directly to Marvin's V.I.P. Section.

Marvin met Pauleena, and her security at the front of the V.I.P with at least twenty goons behind him. "Wassup?" He asked turning up his bottle.

"That's what I came to find out" Pauleena said removing her dark shades. "I been hearing a lot of shit in the streets, and decided I should come down, and hear it from the horses mouth."

"Number one" Marvin began. "You should be thankful I allowed you to come up in here on my bday, and ask me anything, but I'm in a good mood tonight so i'mma let that slide" he paused. "Number two I don't know what you been hearing in the streets, and honestly I don't give a fuck!

This is my city, so if you want the crown you gon have to shoot it off my fucking head!"

Pauleena smiled as she put her shades back on. "That's all I needed to hear thank you for your time" she said politely as her and her security turned and made their way over towards the bar.

"That's what the fuck I'm talking about!" Moonie said all hyped up. "I'm tired of that bitch walking around like she running something. I say we turn it up in here on her tonight."

"Let's enjoy the rest of the night" Marvin smiled as he patted Moonie on the back as he walked over to join the rest of his crew. When Pauleena reached the bar Malcolm ordered her a bottle of Rosay.

"So what you wanna do about this clown?" Malcolm asked.

"He wants to go to war, so we going to take him to war" Pauleena said in an even tone as she sipped on her champagne. "He thinks because I'm a woman, I'm supposed to bow down."

"We both know that ain't happening" Malcolm laughed, as he saw Romelo walking up. The rest of Pauleena's security quickly formed a circle around her once Romelo was in striking distance. "He's cool" she announced.

"Hey Pauleena what you doing up in here?" Romelo asked as he leaned in and kissed her on the cheek.

"Just came through to have a quick word with your son and to enjoy this wonderful party."

"Oh really?" Romelo said with a raised brow." And how did that go?

Pauleena smiled as she took another sip of her champagne. "He asked for a war, so I suggest you get ready to find a nice church."

"Don't go too far, that's still my son" Romelo reminded her.

"That sounds like a personal problem" Pauleena replied with a plain face.

"Let me go try to talk to him before this shit gets out of hand" Romelo said turning headed towards the V.I.P. Section. The last thing he wanted his son mixed up in was an unnecessary war, especially one that could be prevented. Pauleena watched as Romelo disappeared through the crowd. She just shook her head as she continued to sip on her champagne. She knew that Marvin's mind was made up, he had made his bed, now he was going to have to sleep in it.

"How you wanna play this boss?" Malcolm asked looking over the crowd.

"We gon bring it to this bitch, and his whole crew" Pauleena said in mid-sip. "Since he wanna play with the big boys."

"Good cause I didn't like that cat too tough anyway" Malcolm cosigned.

"Text Eraser Head, Roy, and the rest of the goons, and let em know it's on, and to get down here quick."

Marvin sat in between two beautiful women enjoying himself when he noticed his father storm into the V.I.P section with a confused look on his face. "I need to speak to you...now!" Romelo huffed dismissing the two women so the two could speak in private.

"What's on ya mind?" Marvin asked in an uninterested tone as he downed the rest of his drink in one gulp.

"Have you lost your mind?" Romelo barked getting all up in his son's face. "Why the fuck would you start a war with Pauleena without speaking to me first? Are you trying to get yourself killed?"

"I'm tired of playing with this bitch" Marvin said dryly. "If you wanna praise her, then go ahead, not me"

"Pauleena is a powerful woman" Romelo began. "And I think....."

"Fuck what you think!" Marvin snapped cutting his father off. "And fuck Pauleena. Sometimes I wonder what side you on!" As Marvin went to walk away, Romelo firmly grabbed his arm. "Don't you ever in your life talk to me like that!" He said pointing a finger at Marvin. "You are my son, and I just don't want to see nothing bad happen to you!"

Marvin stood there listening to what his father had to say, when he spotted Nancy, and her friend enter the club. "I knew she was feeling me" he said to himself as the words his father spoke went in one ear, and out the other. Once Romelo was done talking, Marvin smoothly walked off heading in Nancy's direction. He figured since she was at his party, then she had to be there to see him.

Nancy stood over in the corner while Coco went to get them some drinks. She didn't go out to clubs often, cause she hated having drunk strange men pulling, and grabbing at her all night. Nancy thought that standing over in the corner would take some of the attention off of her tight fitting red tube dress, but when she looked up, and saw a guy wearing a fake Gucci outfit two stepping towards her she knew her plan had failed. The man swayed back and forth to the beat as he reached for Nancy's hands. "Come on baby" the man smiled flashing a mouth full of fake gold teeth. "I can't just let you stand over in the corner all night."

"Chill" Nancy smiled as she pulled her hands away. "I don't really feel like dancing right now."

"Come on baby" the man pressed. "Don't act like that" he said grabbing her by the waist pulling her closer to him.

"Yo back the fuck up" Nancy said raising her voice as she pushed the man up off of her.

"Fuck you then!" The man yelled in Nancy's face as he turned and walked away. "Stuck up bitch!"

"You a'ight over here?" Coco asked handing Nancy a Long Island iced tea.

"Yeah I'm fine" Nancy replied taking a big sip from her drink. "That's just why I don't like going out. Niggaz don't know how to take no for an answer."

"I see you made it" Marvin said interrupting the two's conversation. It was his party, so he could care less about what the two women were talking about, all that mattered to him was Nancy. He had to have her, and the fact that she wasn't really showing interest only made him want her even more.

"Yeah, my girl drug me out the house tonight" Nancy said. "But since I'm here happy birthday!"

"Imma give you two some privacy" Coco smiled as she disappeared in the crowd leaving the two alone.

"How you feeling tonight" Marvin asked sipping from his bottle as he checked Nancy out from head to toe, everything about her screamed wifey.

"I'm okay" Nancy said looking over at the man wearing the fake Gucci outfit. "That clown over there just tried to ruin my night but I'm fine."

Marvin turned his neck around and saw a man wearing a fake Gucci outfit. "Who him?"

"Yeah him" Nancy sucked her teeth. Marvin waved over a few of his goons who stood close by, and whispered something in one of their ears. Nancy watched as his goons destroyed the man wearing the fake Gucci outfit. One of Marvin's goons stole on the man knocking him out cold, while the rest of the goons tried to stomp him through the floor.

While the goons were putting in work, Marvin continued on with his conversation as if nothing was happening. "I bet he won't be bothering you again" he smiled, as the bouncers finally came and broke up the altercation.

"Thank you but you didn't have to do all that" Nancy said as she watched the bouncers carry the man with the fake Gucci outfit out of the club.

"You disrespect one of my people's, and that's what happens" Marvin shrugged his shoulders as he grabbed Nancy's hand and lead her over towards the V.I.P section. At first Nancy thought that

Marvin was just a regular street nigga, but after talking to him for a while she realized that he was just a business man, with a good heart.

"So what's the deal with you?" Marvin asked draping his arm around Nancy's neck. "Cause you ain't been tryna give a brother no play."

"I told you I had a man" Nancy reminded him.

"Yes, and I invited both of y'all to my party so where is he? And what kind of man would send his beautiful lady out alone anyway?"

"My man couldn't make it today, because he's locked up right now unfortunately" Nancy told him. "But I'm loyal to him, and he knows that I'll never disrespect him."

"You a true down ass bitch" Marvin said. "And I respect that, we need more sisters like you out here, but I know you not gon just be holding down some corny nigga, so who is this lucky man if you don't mind me asking?"

"His name is Ali, and that's my boo" Nancy said pouring herself another drink.

"You talking about Ali that used to run with G-Money?" Marvin smiled. "Yeah I heard some good stories about that brother.....I also heard he got life."

"Yes he does have life, but we promised not to let nothing come in between us....."

"I respect that" Marvin said cutting her off. "But I don't really want to talk about him. Instead I want to talk about our new friendship."

"We can be friends, I don't see no harm in that" Nancy replied.

Moonie sat over in the corner watching Santana's every move. She hated to admit it but she was really feeling him, after the two had sex. She was just going to brush him off, but Santana hit her with the G telling her how he was different, and just because he was a little younger than her didn't mean anything, then out the blue she stopped hearing from him. "This nigga gon make me kill his ass up in here tonight" Moonie said to herself as she watched Santana mingling with a pack of Asian girls. She knew he was a ladies man from the beginning, but now he was her man or at least she thought. Moonie decided to go to the bathroom, and go pee before she did something stupid because the more she watched Santana, the madder she became. As Moonie squeezed through the crowd she rolled her eyes as she passed Pauleena and her team. As Moonie tried to squeeze through the crowd, Pauleena stuck out her foot, and tripped Moonie up. Moonie stumbled before catching her balance. She quickly spun around, and swung on Pauleena. Malcolm caught Moonie's hand in mid air, and then shoved her backwards into the crowd.

Marvin sat up in the V.I.P talking to Nancy when he saw The Terminator walked up in the V.I.P. "Happy bday my G" he greeted Marvin with a pound followed by a hug.

"What's up champ?" Marvin smiled as he handed The Terminator a drink. "I got somebody I want you to meet. This right here is my friend Nancy."

"Oh we've met already" Nancy said in a nasty tone cutting her eyes at the champ. She didn't like how he had treated Coco when the two were dating. She didn't respect men who treated their woman like they were underneath them especially after what she had went through with Dave.

"Yeah I've seen her around before" The Terminator said in a nonchalant tone. Before Marvin got a chance to say another word, he saw a light scuffle break out on the dance floor.

"Yo that's Moonie!" One of his goons announced as everybody ran over there to see what was going on.

"Don't be a punk bitch" Moonie yelled. "Let's get it on right now me and you one on one!"

Pauleena smirked as she tossed her drink in Moonie's face. She was above fighting the hood rat in the club, but if she had to she would gladly beat the bitch's ass where ever she stood.

Once the drink splashed in Moonie's face and weave, she went crazy, but once again Pauleena's security stopped Moonie from getting at her.

Marvin walked up on the scene and snatched the Muslim's hands off of Moonie. The Muslim quickly charged at Marvin, but before he could reach him The Terminator had already caught him with a two piece knocking him out cold. Once one of the security hit the floor, Malcolm was already in motion. He grabbed The Terminator in a bear hug and lifted him up in the air, just as he was about to dump him on his head, Marvin put a bullet in his leg. "POW!!" The gun shot sent the club in a frenzy as people climbed over top of each other trying to get out of the club. Once Malcolm hit the floor Smitty and the rest of Marvin's goons stomped him out. Marvin aimed his gun at Pauleena, and pulled the trigger. One of Pauleena's security guards jumped in front of the bullet for his boss while her last two guards quickly rushed her towards the club's exit. In the mist of everything Pauleena managed to pull her .380 from her purse, and fired two rounds in the direction of all the commotion. One of the bullets ripped through Marvin's shoulder causing him to drop his gun, and hit the floor. Smitty and the rest of Marvin's goons opened fire on Pauleena once they saw Marvin hit the floor. Pauleena's last two security guards quickly rushed her up out of the club. When Pauleena made it outside she saw Eraser Head and Roy positioned in the parking lot, both men holding assault riffles.

"Air this whole shit out!" Pauleena ordered as she continued on towards her ride. Roy smiled as him, and Eraser Head riddled the front of the club with bullets, hitting every, and anybody in sight. A smirk danced on Pauleena's lips when she heard the gun fire erupt as her driver pulled out of the parking lot. Once Roy, and Eraser Head ran out of bullets, they quickly hopped back in there car, and burnt rubber.

Inside the club Smitty and another goon helped Marvin outside where a car waited curb side. Marvin smoothly slid in the back seat. "I got it from here fam" Smitty said as he snatched the driver out the front seat, and took his place. Once Smitty was sure Marvin was okay he pulled out of the parking lot like a mad man. "Hang in there my nigga" Smitty said out loud. "We'll be at the hospital in no time."

"It's on now!" Marvin yelled from the back seat. He still couldn't believe that Pauleena had shot him, for that she would definitely have to pay with her life. "Did y'all kill that ugly Muslim security guard?"

"Damn near" Smitty chuckled.

"This bitch want a war, then that's just what she going to get" Marvin said with his eyes closed in obvious pain.

"Damn!" Smitty said peeking through the rearview mirror. "Cops pulling us over, what you want me to do?"

"Pull over real quick, and tell them clowns you taking me to the hospital" Marvin replied, as he felt the car pulling over to the side of the road. "What them mufucka's doing?"

"They just sitting there" Smitty replied watching the unmarked car through the rearview mirror. "They probably running the plates." Seconds later Detective Nelson stepped out of the unmarked car, and slowly made his way towards the car. "Good evening gentlemen" Detective Nelson said with an evil smile on his face. "You guys seem to be in a rush is everything alright?" He asked as another squad car pulled up to the scene.

"I'm just trying to get my partner to the hospital" Smitty said with urgency in his voice. "What did I do wrong?"

"Step out the car for a second sir" Detective Nelson ordered.

"Why what did I do?" Smitty questioned not budging. He was used to being harassed by the police, so he made sure he always gave them a hard time every time they stopped him. Detective Nelson quickly snapped open the driver door, and stuck his taser to Smitty's ribs. Smitty's body shook like he was having a seizure as Detective Nelson dragged him out the vehicle.

"Fuck is y'all niggaz doing?" Marvin yelled from the back seat as he watched the detective taser Smitty and snatched him out the car. Before he could say another word the back door shot open, and a uniform cop snatched him out the back seat, cuffed him, and left him laying face down on the ground.

Detective Nelson slowly walked over towards where Marvin laid face down on the ground, and kneeled down so the wounded man could hear him. "Listen carefully you little bitch" he slipped a cigarette in his mouth and lit it before he continued. "I want my money, and the longer it takes you to get me my money, the more you going to have to see my face" he blew rings of smoke down in Marvin's face. "And trust me this is the last face you want to see everyday" he warned.

"I need to go to the hospital, I've been shot" Marvin said wincing in pain. He'd been shot in the shoulder, and his hands being cuffed behind his back wasn't helping. "Please" he begged.

A smirk appeared on Detective Nelson's face as he pulled his taser from his back pocket, and jabbed into Marvin's neck. He laughed as Marvin's body shook uncontrollably.

"What the fuck is going on over here!" A voice yelled from behind Detective Nelson. Detective Nelson turned around and saw Romelo hopping out of his truck. "Take yo mufucking hands off of my son!" He barked.

"What you going to do if I don't?" Detective Nelson challenged as he walked straight up to Romelo.

"My son needs to get to a hospital" Romelo said pulling out a wad of cash, and holding it out.

"Tell that idiot son of yours to stop testing me" Detective Nelson said as he snatched the money out of Romelo's hand. "The next time I won't be so nice" he said as he walked off.

"Can I at least have the keys so I can uncuff them?" Romelo asked as he watched the detective pull off ignoring his last question.

"I swear to god I'm going to kill that cracker!" Smitty growled from the ground. Romelo struggled getting Marvin and Smitty to their feet and in the back of his truck being that both men hands were still cuffed behind their backs.

"I'm going to make sure Detective Nelson gets what he got coming to him" Marvin said out loud. "But first" he said turning to look at Smitty. "I want you to put the word out $100,000 to whomever puts a bullet in that bitch Pauleena's head!"

"You sure that's a good idea to go at both of them at the same time?" Romelo asked peeking at the two men through the rearview mirror.

"No disrespect pops, but right now I'm going to need you to mind your business" Marvin told him, and the conversation was left at that.

* * *

"Hard Time"

Ali sat in the day room playing spades, bobbing his head to the music that played on the small commissary radio. He tried to keep his mind off of Nancy, but that was a job easier said than done. It seemed the more he tried not to think about her the more she ran across his mind.

"Damn!" An inmate with scrappy looking corn rows said as he saw C.O. Crystal heading in their direction. "I don't fuck with no police, but I'd tear her ass up" he said with a thirsty look in his eyes.

"Keep it real with us Ali you be busting her ass don't you?" A diesel inmate asked.

"Nah" Ali lied. "I don't trust no police, the last time I trusted a police it landed me up in here" he said as he watched every step that Crystal took. Crystal approached the card game. Her ass looked like it was going to rip through the uniform pants any second. "Hey Ali can I have a word with you for a second?"

Ali walked over to the side where he and Crystal spoke in hushed voices.

"I need you to break me off" Crystal said with a seductive look in her eyes.

"Set it up and you know I'll be there" Ali replied as he looked around, and noticed that all eyes were on them. "Listen you gon have to start getting in contact with me a little more discreetly, you know one of these jealous clowns will drop dime on us in a heartbeat."

"I got you baby" Crystal replied looking around noticing all the attention they were getting. "But the real reason I came down here was to tell you that I heard from a snitch, that Big Blood, and a few of his boys were planning on shanking you if you went to the yard today."

"Word?" Ali asked.

"That's the word going around" Crystal said. "What did you do to him, that's got him so pissed off at you?"

"I have no idea" Ali replied honestly.

"I gotta go you just make sure you be careful, i'll set something up for us sometime this week baby" she said walking off leaving Ali standing there.

"Everything good?" Skip asked walking over to where Ali stood.

"She just told me that clown Big Blood is telling everybody it's on if I come to the yard" Ali chuckled.

"Say word" Skip said not believing what he just heard.

"Word" Ali said as he and Skip made their way over to his cell. Under Ali's mattress he pulled out two shanks. "This nigga must think it's a game" he said handing Skip a shank. Skip quickly rounded up a couple of goons, before he, Ali, and the goons made their way out to the yard.

Out in the yard Big Blood, and a bunch of blood niggaz stood over by the pull up bars looking for trouble. Big Blood wanted his name to be the most talked about in the jail. He lived to put in work. The word on the street was that Ali was the man when he was out on the streets so he figured he'd make a name for himself by going at Ali. Not to mention he had heard that G-Money was the wild one out the crew, and Ali was the peaceful one, that alone made Big Blood want to go at Ali even more.

Ali stepped foot in the yard, and immediately all eyes were on him. In jail news traveled fast, and every inmate already knew something big was about to jump off. Ali and his crew strolled through the yard looking for Big Blood and his crew. As Ali strolled through the yard, an old head nodded his head in the direction that Big Blood was in. Ali winked back at the old head, and headed straight towards the pull up bars. When Big Blood saw Ali and his crew approaching he immediately met him half way.

"Heard you was looking for me?" Ali asked with one hand in his pocket.

"Nigga I don't like you" Big Blood said pointing his finger in Ali's face. Before Ali could make a move Skip jumped in, and snuffed Big Blood. Instantly the two crews clashed.

Big Blood pulled his shank out from out his pocket, as he, and Ali went knife for knife in the middle of the yard. Ali swung his shank at Big Blood causing him to jump back.

"Come on you pussy let's see what you got" Big Blood said with a wicked grin as he and Ali faced off. Big Blood launched at Ali trying to jab his shank in his chest, Ali quickly jumped back, and sliced Big Blood on the wrist causing him to drop his knife. Before Ali could go in for the kill two big C.O.'s jumped on his back roughly tackling him to the ground. While Ali laid face down on the ground Big Blood ran over, and got in a few cheap kicks before he too was tossed to the ground by the police.

"This shit ain't over muthafucka!" Big Blood yelled as two C.O.'s escorted him out of the yard, and back inside the prison. As Ali laid on the ground he looked up, and saw Crystal looking at him. She mouthed the words. "Are you okay?"

Ali replied with a wink as the C.O.'s snatched him up off the ground, and escorted him, and his crew back inside.
***

"How Real Can It Get"

Pauleena stepped out the shower butt naked. She quickly dried herself with a towel before she exited the bathroom. She was still pissed that Marvin, and his crew had the balls to try to make a move on her at the club. But what really had her mad was the fact that, that bum ass chick Moonie had tried to stunt on her like she was built like that. "Next time I see that bum bitch, imma show her something" Pauleena said to herself as she got dressed. She threw on an expensive custom made black woman's business suit. Every Saturday she got her hair done at the same shop, not out of habit, but because Jessica her Spanish hair stylist was the only one that knew how to do her long hair the way she liked it. Pauleena threw on her shoulder holster, slid her two .380's down in the holster, put her blazer over top, and headed out the door. Since Malcolm was in the hospital, nursing his gun shot wound Pauleena was forced to use another Muslim security guard named Jihad. Jihad wasn't as big as Malcolm but he was definitely a protector, and a good body guard. Pauleena, Jihad, and two other Muslim guards hopped in an all black Denali.

In the parking lot in front of the beauty palor Smitty and Moonie had been staked out in a hooptie since sun rise. "One of my Dominican homegirls told me this is where Pauleena comes to get her hair done every Saturday" Moonie said as she clutched the Tec-9 that rested on her lap.

"I hope so" Smitty huffed. He couldn't believe Pauleena had actually shot Marvin in his shoulder. With him being the head of Marvin's security, that didn't make him look too good, and now he was out to redeem himself by any means necessary.

"Can you believe how the bitch tried to front on me in the club?" Moonie huffed. "If her punk ass security wasn't there I would of washed her up!" Moonie was about to finish her rant until she spotted a black Denali creep up in the parking lot. "Be on point I think this is her right here pulling up" Moonie said in a serious tone. Smitty and Moonie both looked on closely as they watched the Denali's every move.

Jihad pulled up directly in front of the beauty salon, and left the engine running as he hopped out, and walked around to the back of the truck, and opened the door for Pauleena. The other two security guards hopped out the truck scanning the parking lot as their boss hopped out the back seat. Pauleena's heels hit the concrete with confidence. She took only six steps before she heard gun fire. Immediately Jihad tackled Pauleena to the ground, and covered her with his own body, while her other two security guards had a shoot out in broad day light with the gunmen.

Moonie aimed her Tec-9 at one of Pauleena's security guards, and squeezed the trigger. The machine gun rattled in her hands as the bullets ripped through the first guard's body effortlessly. The other body guard tried to take cover behind the truck, but a bullet grazed his face causing his body to drop, and hit the concrete hard.

"Get the fuck off me!" Pauleena screamed as she pushed Jihad up off of her. She quickly kicked off her heels, and snatched her two .380's from her holsters, as she crept over to her truck for cover.

"Nah bitch don't try to hide now!" Moonie yelled as she opened fire on the truck rocking it back, and forth. Pauleena ducked down, as broken glass rained down on top of her head.

"Boss I'm going to distract them" Jihad said with a scared look in his eyes. "You hop in the car, and take off while I do that."

Pauleena replied with a head nod. Three seconds later Jihad sprang up from behind the truck, busting his 9mm. Pauleena quickly hopped in the driver seat of the truck, as she watched the gunmen riddle Jihad's body with bullets. The two gunmen then quickly ran towards the front of Pauleena's truck, and opened fire.

"Shit!" Pauleena cursed, as she threw the gear in reverse, and stomped on the gas peddal, she ducked down as several bullets exploded through the front windshield. Smitty and Moonie slowly walked towards the truck popping shot after shot as it backed away out of control.

Pauleena kept her head down and her foot on the gas, until the truck crashed into something making a loud bang. Smitty and Moonie reloaded their weapons, as they moved closer to the truck. Pauleena kept her head down until she heard the gun fire stop, she quickly reached down, and grabbed her two .380's from off the floor. "Y'all wanna fuck with me!?" She yelled as she opened fire from the inside of her truck. POW, POW, POW, POW, POW, POW!!! Once she saw the two gunmen scrambling for cover, she quickly hopped out the truck, and took off on foot. Pauleena ran down the street bare foot, with a gun in each hand yelling for help.

Moonie was about to chase Pauleena, until Smitty stopped her. "We gotta go!" He said with a tight grip on her shirt. Moonie didn't want to hear it, but Smitty was right if they didn't leave now, they would definitely be seeing the inside of a jail cell for a long time.

"Fuck!" Moonie cursed loudly out of frustration as she, and Smitty ran back to their car, and peeled off.

Pauleena ran out into the middle of the street causing cars to come to a hault. The bottoms of her feet were on fire, but she ignored the pain and kept on sprinting. Pauleena ran straight inside Burger King where she ran straight to the bathroom.

"Somebody's in here!" A lady yelled when the bathroom door snatched open. The butt of Pauleena's gun quickly silenced the woman knocking her out cold. Pauleena stepped over the woman's body as she wiped her prints off the guns, as she removed the top piece off the back of the toilet, and dropped the guns down in the top. Put the lid back on top, then left like nothing ever happened. Pauleena went outside, and called someone to come, and pick her up. While she waited the only thing that was on her mind were murderous thoughts. She couldn't believe that Marvin had tried to take her out in broad daylight, and had her running for her life bare foot. A situation like this called for desperate measures Pauleena quickly pulled her cell phone back out, and made a call to one of the most ruthless killers she knew in Miami. On the third ring a raspy voice answered the phone. "Good evening" he answered.

"Hey Paco it's Pauleena" she told him.

"Pauleena?" Paco chuckled. "Last I heard you was out in New York running shit, how you been?"

"Not too good" Pauleena replied as her ride pulled up. "Some new jacks just tried to take me out in broad daylight."

"Broad daylight?" Paco echoed.

"Broad daylight" Pauleena repeated as she hopped in her ride. "Paco I need you."

"I'll be there first thing in the morning just have somebody there to pick me up from the airport" Paco said ending the call. Paco was the most ruthless hit man out in Miami. He made a name for himself by always going over board on his targets.

Paco and Pauleena had grown up a few blocks away from each other. He knew if she was calling him then it had to be serious. Paco smiled as he began to pack a light bag. He wasn't sure if New York was ready for what he was about to bring, but ready or not he was on his way.

* * *

"Surprise, Surprise"

Nancy got Lil Ali dressed, as Alicia Keys hummed softly in the background. She was taking Lil man out to the park so he could get some fresh air. She still couldn't believe what had went down at the club last week. That's the reason why she rather stay in the house instead of in some jammed packed club, you never knew what might happen when so many ignorant people ended up in one spot. She was just happy that she and Coco had made it out of the club in one piece. Nancy was packing a small bag for Lil Ali when she heard her door bell ring. She walked over to the door, and opened it without looking through the peephole thinking it was Coco, she was shocked when she saw who was on the other side of the door. "Hey um what are you doing here?" Nancy asked.

"Sorry for just popping up like this" Marvin apologized standing there with his arm in a sling. "I just came by to apologize for what happened the other night in the club. I want you to know that's not how I get down. Some unexpected shit just jumped off."

"Listen Marvin" Nancy said not believing a word he spoke. "You are in the street life, and that's what happens. People want to kill you for any reason, so save all your apologies. It is what it is!"

"Let me make it up to you" Marvin offered. "Let me take you to get something to eat."

"You can't be serious" Nancy laughed in his face. "You expect me to go out with you, and risk getting my head blown off again?"

"I promise you things will be different" Marvin told her. "I'll never put you in harms way again" Nancy looked over Marvin's shoulder and saw Smitty, and another rough looking man leaning on the hood of Marvin's Lexus.

"What do you want from me?" Nancy asked.

"I just want to spend a lil time with you, that's all" Marvin told her.

"I already told you I got a man" Nancy reminded him. "And I don't think he would appreciate me hanging out with you."

"Ali ain't never getting out of jail" Marvin said. "And plus I'm not asking you to marry me, I just want to hang out and spend a lil time with you" he pressed.

"Thanks, but no thanks" Nancy said kindly.

"A'ight ma I guess I'll see you around" Marvin said as he turned and headed back towards his Lexus, and hopped in the back seat.

Nancy stood in the door way until the Lexus was out of site. Marvin was definitely handsome, and her type, but she was loyal to Ali even if he did have life.

"Mommy I gotta pee" Lil Ali said running off towards the bathroom. Nancy smiled as she watched her lil man sprint towards the bathroom. She was about to join him in the bathroom until she heard her door bell ring again. "Didn't I just tell this Nigga I got a man?" Nancy said out loud as she walked back over to the door, and opened it. On the other side of the door stood Christie.

"Oh shit!" Nancy said covering her mouth with her hand. The last time she had seen Christie the girl was damn near on her death bed from fucking with that crack, now the Christie that stood before her was the Christie of normal before Spanky died, and before the crack.

"Hey girl" Christie said flashing a bright smile, as she leaned in for a hug. Nancy hugged Christie back as her eyes began to water. It felt good to see her friend get her life back on the right track, especially after being so far gone.

"Girl get in here" Nancy said stepping to the side so Christie could enter. "I'm so happy you finally got yourself together."

"It wasn't easy girl, but I had to do what I had to do" Christie said with a smile. "And with the help of God anything is possible"

"I know that's right" Nancy agreed. "So what have you been doing with yourself?" She asked as the two took a seat on the leather sofa.

"I met this wonderful man while I was in rehab" Christie boasted. "I mean he's the absolute best, through all my problems he never left my side, and help push me through it praise Jesus.

"That's great" Nancy said skeptically. "So you met this new guy in rehab?"

"Yeah his name is Romelo, and I didn't actually meet him in rehab, I kind of met him while I was trying to escape from the facility. And it was him that talked me into going back, and getting the help I needed" Christie paused. "He came to the rehab everyday to make sure I was good."

"Sounds like a keeper" Nancy smiled. She was just happy that Christie had gotten her life back on the right track. "Can't wait to meet him."

"He's a little older than me, but I love the way he treats me" Christie explained.

"I feel you" Nancy smiled wiping the tears from her eyes. "I was just about to take Lil Ali to the park would you like to join us?"

"Sure I would love to" Christie said as she, Nancy and Lil Ali headed out to the park to catch up on old times.

***

Tears of a Hustler 3

"Welcome Back"

Knowledge sat in his condo in Philly, watching the NBA playoffs getting his drink on. In his new life all he did was stay in the house most of the time staying low and off the police's radar. He didn't really like or enjoy living like this, but he had to do what he had to do. Knowledge missed living the fast life, and sometimes he found himself thinking about G-Money back when he was a nobody. It was G-Money who had given him the opportunity to become a known Nigga, and to make some money. Knowledge poured himself another glass of Coconut Ciroc when he heard a noise coming from by the front door. He quickly grabbed his .380 from off the coffee table, and headed towards the front door to investigate. When Knowledge reached the living room, and saw who was standing there he immediately lowered his weapon.

Pauleena stood in Knowledge's living room along with four of her Muslim body guards with a smile on her face.

"What you doing here?" Knowledge asked as he walked over and gave her a hug.

"I need you" Pauleena said cutting straight to the chase. "I need a good soldier like you on my team, shit getting real out here in the streets."

Knowledge took a swig from his glass before he replied. "Nah I'm out the game, I ain't put in no work in mad long, plus you know I'm a wanted man."

"Fuck the police" Pauleena huffed walking over helping herself to a drink. "You told me if I ever needed you, all I had to do was holla, and right now I need you more then ever."

"I don't know" Knowledge hesitated. He knew what Pauleena was asking him to do, and he had to admit that the life he was living was the most boring life ever. Truth be told he missed the action, and more importantly he missed the fast life.

"Some new clowns out here running around thinking they the shit" Pauleena smiled. "I need you to come show these fools how it's really done."

Knowledge smiled. "Give me a little time to think everything over."

"No fuck that!" Pauleena spat. "I need to know right now. Are you in or out!?"

Knowledge sat there for a second, as he took a few more sips from his glass. "Fuck it I'm in."

Pauleena sat $40,000 down in front of Knowledge. "Go get dress we got work to do. " Knowledge picked up the money and examined it for a second before heading upstairs to get the rest of his things. Pauleena sat on the couch enjoying a drink while Knowledge went to get dressed. She knew with him on her side a lot of things were going to be different, she needed a live wire on her team, someone who just didn't give a fuck about nothing, and Knowledge was her man. Besides he was trained by G-Money therefore she knew he could be trusted.

On the ride back to New York Pauleena told Knowledge all about Marvin, and his crew, and how they had her running down the street dodging bullets bare foot. She also told Knowledge about the crazy hit man Paco that she had coming to New York in the morning.

"I see a lot of things have changed since I've been gone" Knowledge said putting fire to the end of his blunt. "But don't worry once I get back I'll get things back under control" he assured her.

"These clowns wanna fuck with me?" Pauleena said out loud. "They fucking with the right one!" For the rest of the ride Pauleena brought Knowledge up to speed on everything that has been going on, and everything he had missed while he was gone. When Pauleena's security pulled up in front of her mansion they saw a man standing directly in front of the front door. The man wore a pair of jeans, cowboy boots, and a button up shirt. The top three buttons on his shirt were unbuttoned exposing his hairy chest, along with the three thin gold chains that rested on top of the taco meat. The man had long hair that came down to his shoulders, and on his face he sported a rugged looking beard.

"Fuck is this clown in front of your door?" Knowledge asked.

"That's my main man Paco" Pauleena said with a smile as she exited the vehicle heading towards the well known killer. "Glad you could make it on such short notice."

"Come on" Paco said opening his arms for a hug. "You know whenever you call me I'll be there no questions asked."

"Paco this right here is my man Knowledge, Knowledge meet Paco" she introduced the two. Knowledge and Paco shook hands quickly before all three of them went inside. Pauleena lead them through the house, and into her office.

"So who are these men that's been giving you so much trouble?" Paco asked in broken English.

"Some faggot named Marvin" Pauleena huffed as she handed him a folder with pictures of Marvin, and all the top members in his organization. "I need you to hunt each and every one of those mufucka's down, and kill em!"

"My pleasure" Paco replied as he studied the folder.

"What you need me to do?" Knowledge asked.

"I just need you to hold me down" Pauleena told him. "You going to be kind of like my body guard where ever I go....you go!"

"I got you" Knowledge said. In his mind he felt this would be the easiest job he ever had.

"While Paco is taking care of that" Pauleena said looking over at Knowledge. "I got something me, and you need to go take care of."

***

"The Box"

C.O. Crystal sat at her desk, and watched as Ali played cards with a few other inmates. It had been a while since the last time they had sex, and she desperately needed to feel him inside of her. Since Ali had been in the box because of the scuffle that he and Big Blood had, it been hard for Crystal to sneak him away for a piece of action. Her main focus now was to keep Ali out of any trouble, before the warden decided to ship him off to another jail. As Crystal sat there keeping a close eye on all the inmates she heard some music blasting coming from one of the cells on the top tier. A white C.O. sighed loudly as he raised from his seat.

"Don't worry about it Bob" Crystal told him. "I got this." She got up from her chair, and headed up stairs to see who was blasting their music like they were crazy. The closer Crystal got the louder she heard Rick Ross's song "John Doe" when Crystal finally reached the cell where the music was coming from, she looked inside, and saw Big Blood in his cell with no shirt on lifting a laundry bag full of books.

"Um excuse me!" She yelled over the music. "I said excuse me!" Big Blood continued on with his work out like he didn't hear her. Crystal walked in his cell, and tapped him on the shoulder.

"What the fuck do you want?" Big Blood said in a bored tone not even bothering to turn around, and face her.

"Turn your music down right now!" Crystal yelled.

"When I finish working out" Big Blood replied dryly. Crystal looked at him like he was insane. She then walked over, and hit the stop button on his radio. "Mufucka I said to turn this shit off now!"

Big Blood spun around, and back slapped Crystal across her face sending her stumbling out of his cell. He then ran, and clothes lined her over the rail. Ali and the rest of the inmates watched as they saw C.O. Crystal fall from the top tier all the way down to the floor. Big Blood looked down at Crystal's body sprawled out on the floor, and laughed like it was funny. He then looked down at Ali, and winked at him. Seconds later Big Blood was tackled by a gang of C.O.s. The rest of the inmates watched as they escorted him to the box kicking, and screaming.

***

"The Champ Is Here"

The Terminator dripped with sweat as he went to work on the speed bag. He had a good rhythm going. All the noise from other boxers working out in the gym made the champ feel like he was the king. Lately he'd been focused because he had another big fight coming up in two months. His trainer and advisor Mr. Wilson had been on his back lately about all the partying, and all the bad decisions he'd been making lately. Mr. Wilson saw that his fighter was hanging out with the wrong crowd, and he knew nothing positive would come from that. The front door to the gym opened, and the entire gym went silent. Knowledge entered the gym followed by Pauleena, along with two Muslim guards on her heels. Everyone looked on as Pauleena's heels rang loudly on the wood floor. The Terminator stopped hitting the speed bag as he watched Pauleena, and her crew heading in his direction.

"I'm sorry" Mr. Wilson said stepping in front of Pauleena and her crew, "but this gym is closed to outsiders."

Knowledge's hand quickly shot out as he punched Mr. Wilson in his face dropping the old man off impact. "Who the fuck asked you anything!?"

Pauleena stepped over Mr. Wilson's body as she walked up to The Terminator.

"What's this all about?" The Terminator asked with a nervous look on his face.

"This is about you sticking your nose in my business the other night at the club" Pauleena said with a smirk on her face. She smoothly pulled a .380 from her shoulder holster, and let it dangle at her side.

The Terminator looked down at the gun, and threw his hands up in surrender. "Listen I'm sorry about what happened the other night, everything happened so fast, and I was just trying to hold my man down on his bday" he said copping a plea. Pauleena raised her gun, and pointed it at the man standing next to The Terminator, and shot him in the leg. "POW" "It look like I give a fuck about ya man bday?" She asked pointing the gun at The Terminator.

"It was a mistake" The Terminator replied with fear in his eyes.

"Listen you got two choices" Pauleena said with a smile. "One I can pull this trigger right now, and kill you, or two in your next fight you can take a dive."

"Take a dive?" The Terminator repeated. "Why would I do something like that?"

"Because I'm going to bet a million dollars on your next opponent, and you're going to take a dive" Pauleena smiled. "If you don't take a dive, then I'll have you murdered within twenty four hours after the fight. The choice is yours."

"So what's it going to be?" Knowledge chimed in from the side line hoping The Terminator decided to play tough so he could get revenge on him for knocking him out a while back.

"Listen" The Terminator began. "I don't know how to lose, if you want to win some money, then just bet on me" he said as if it was that simple.

Pauleena aimed her gun at the heavy bag, and pulled the trigger to let everyone in the gym know she wasn't fucking around. "Listen you silly mufucka" Pauleena said tired of debating, she wasn't asking him she was telling him. "Either you going to take the dive, or not now what's it going to be?" She asked pointing her .380 at his head.

"I'll take the dive" The Terminator said in a low voice looking down at the floor. Losing was something he wasn't accustomed to.

"It was nice doing business with you, I'll be in touch" Pauleena smiled as she turned, and walked off.

"Next tim, learn how to mind your business" Knowledge said looking the The Terminator up, and down as he gave Mr. Wilson one last kick. The Terminator watched as Pauleena, and her crew strolled up out of his gym. Not knowing what else to do The Terminator reached inside his gym back, removed his cell phone, and called Marvin.

* * *

Paco pulled his car over in front of a KFC at the end of the corner. He been tailing a few of Marvin's main workers all day watching them make pick ups, and drop offs. Paco couldn't stand how arrogant the men were, that alone made him want to kill them even more. He was brought in to send a message out to Marvin, and that's just what planned on doing. Paco watched closely as the four men entered the restaurant. He waited a second before exiting his car, and heading to his trunk. Inside the trunk an A.K. 47 rested on top of a duffle bag. Just as the four men were getting ready to exit the chicken spot Paca whipped the A.K. And let it rip. "Rat, TAT, TAT, TAT, TAT, TAT, TAT!!!!!!" The A.K. rattled in Paco's hands as bullets ripped through his four intended targets, innocent by standers, kids, and a few KFC employees. Once Paco's clip was empty, he tossed the A.K. back in the trunk, slammed it shut, hopped back in the driver seat, and peeled off leaving a trail of dead bodies behind.

* * *

"Where You Been?"

Nancy's heels click, clacked loudly as she walked through the restaurant. She hadn't seen her best friend Coco in a while, and the two decided to meet up for dinner. As Nancy approached the table she noticed Coco at the table sporting a pair of dark shades. She immediately looked at Coco with a suspicious eye. Dark shades on inside Hmmph! Something wasn't right.

"Where the hell have you been?" Nancy asked with a smile, joining Coco at the table. Usually it was Nancy who would always be in the house, not Coco.

"Nothing" Coco replied dryly. "I just been chilling"

"Chilling?" Nancy repeated happy to see her best friend. "I haven't seen, or heard from you since the last time when we were at the club" she reminded her.

"Girl I just been chilling, getting a little me time in" Coco forced a smile on her face, as she took a sip from her water that sat in front of her.

"What's up with those dark shades?" Nancy asked suspiciously.

"Just letting my eyes rest" Coco answered quickly. "How's lil Ali been?" She said quickly changing the subject.

Nancy swiftly reached across the table, and snatched Coco's shades from off of her face. Coco sported a dark ring under her eye. It looked as if she had tried to cover her bruise with lots of make up, but even that didn't cover the bruise.

"What the fuck happened to your eye?" Nancy shook her head in disbelief. "After all the shit you witnessed me go through with Dave, you gon sit back, and let a Nigga use you like a punching bag?"

"It's not even like that" Coco said. "Tony really loves me, this is all my fault, he found a few numbers in my phone, and went crazy."

"You making an excuse for him to do this?" Nancy huffed. "You know damn well once he put his hands on you, that she ain't gon stop, didn't you learn from the mistakes I made!?"

"Tony is nothing like Dave" Coco said in a matter of fact tone. "Tony really loves me. Dave never gave a shit about you."

"If he loved you so much, then why are you walking around with a black eye?" Nancy asked.

Coco shot to her feet. "Since when did you become, a specialist on relationships?" She folded her arms across her chest. "Last time I checked you couldn't even get a Nigga with life in prison to love you, so you might want to get yo own shit together before you come creeping in my backyard!" Coco rolled her eyes and walked off. Nancy followed Coco out into the parking lot. "That's right run home to that Nigga so he can beat yo ass some more!" She yelled. "You so stupid!"

Coco ignored her former friend, and hopped in her Honda Civic, and pulled off leaving Nancy standing there in the parking lot.

"Dummy!" Nancy yelled as she watched her best friend drive off like a mad woman. "Fuck that!" She said out loud as she jogged over to her Lexus, and followed Coco.

"I can't let you go out like that" Nancy said to herself, as she headed towards Coco's crib. She couldn't believe that Coco would let a man put his hands on her, then give her the cold shoulder for telling her what she needed to hear, and not what she wanted to hear. When Nancy pulled up to Coco's house, she saw a man's shadow smacking the shit out of someone from the front window. She sighed loudly, then stepped out of her Lexus, and headed to the front door, and rung the door bell.

Seconds later a man big man snatched the door open. "What the fuck do you want!?" Tony growled.

"Don't put ya fucking hands on my friend again!" Nancy yelled pointing her finger at the big man.

A smirk danced on Tony's lips as he snatched Nancy inside the house, and shut the door behind him. "Bitch!" He barked as he back slapped Nancy to the floor.

"No Tony don't!" Coco begged from the sideline. "She's just trying to help me."

"Good so now you can watch her take your ass whipping!" Tony huffed as he went to work on Nancy. Coco cried her eyes out watching Nancy take the ass whipping from Tony. She wished Nancy would of just minded her own business, and went home instead of following her home. Tony didn't stop until Nancy's face was a bloody mess. "Next time you'll keep your nose out of grown folks business" Tony chuckled as he exited the house, and hopped in the Benz that G-Money had brought for Coco. When he went out he'd always take the Benz, and make Coco drive the Honda.

Once Tony was gone, Coco crawled over to Nancy, and cradled her head in her arms. "I'm so sorry Nancy, I'm so sorry" she cried wishing she had never went out to meet Nancy at the restaurant. She planned on not leaving the house until her bruises were gone, but when Nancy had called her she just couldn't resist, and agreed to meet her at the restaurant for a few drinks. When Coco got back in the house, Tony had accused her of creeping around with another man, and began slapping her around. As Coco thought back on everything that had happened, she wished she would've just sent Nancy's call to the voicemail.

"What's Really Good?"

Moonie moaned passionately as she wrapped her legs around Santana's head. "Don't stop baby!" She continued to moan thrusting her hips up and down grinding her pussy on Santana's face until she finally came. Santana then slid in between Moonie's legs as he slipped right inside of her. He pinned Moonie's legs back to her shoulders and plunged in and out of her walls at a fast pace, until he exploded. Once the two were done Moonie ran to the bathroom, and took a quick shower.

"Get dress we gotta get going" Moonie said lotioning her body.

"What's the rush?" Santana asked laying across the bed naked with his eyes closed.

"Cause Marvin supposed to be having this meeting down at the warehouse" Monnie reminded him.

"Shit" Santana huffed. "I hope this ain't no meeting about that Pauleena chick, I'm tired of hearing about that bitch!"

"The faster we kill that bitch, the faster all this bullshit will be over" Moonie said loading her 9mm. Moonie hated Pauleena, and couldn't wait until the next time the two crossed each other's path. She looked forward to the challenge.

Thirty minutes later Moonie pulled up in front of the warehouse, and saw about thirty to forty goons standing out front. After greeting each soldier Marvin got everyone's attention. "We at war right now" he began. "This bitch Pauleena thinks she can hang with the big boys, so we gon show her what time it is. I don't care where any of you run into her at, I want shots fired on site" Marvin said making sure he made that part clear. Just as Marvin was about to continue his speech he saw a black BMW cruising down the block at a slow pace blasting OJ The Juice Man's song "Make The Trap Ayy."

Knowledge cruised by with one of his Spanish chicks in the front seat, and two of his shooters in the back. "Look at these clowns" he smirked as he grilled each man as the BMW passed.

"Ain't that one of G-Money's boys?" Smitty asked eyeing the BMW.

Marvin pulled his .45 from his waistband, and fired two shots at the BMW. He wasn't sure who the driver of the car was, but he didn't like how they drove past grilling him, and his crew. If it was one of Pauleena's workers he wanted to let em know what time it was.

Knowledge stomped on the brakes after he heard the two shots ring out, him and his crew hopped out the BMW, and opened fire on Marvin's crew. Marvin and his crew returned fire holding court in the middle of the street.

Knowledge and his crew hopped back in the BMW and peeled off. They were out numbered and out gunned. "Don't worry we gon catch them niggaz again" Knowledge said as he hopped on the ramp heading to the highway.

"More money more problems"

Marvin sat over by the bar area in his house having a strong drink. Ever since him, and Pauleena had been beefing he'd noticed that his money began to slow down a bit due to all the heat from the police. In one ear he had his father telling him going to war wasn't good for business, in the other ear were his goons telling him to let them go out and hunt Pauleena down.

"I'm telling you" Romelo said having a seat next to his son. "Your pockets are going to be the only one taking a hit until this stupid war is over." Marvin looked over at his pops like he was crazy. "Listen I know that's your new girl friend, and all that, no disrespect, but I don't know that bitch so don't speak about none of my business in front of her" he said looking over at Christie who sat on the couch.

Christie didn't like Marvin. He looked at her and treated her as if she was an undercover cop or as if she was wearing a wire. This was the fifth time the two were in each other's company and each time he treated her like an outsider.

Marvin knew Christie was his pops new girl friend, but for some reason he didn't like or trust the bitch. Truth be told, he really didn't even want her in his house, but since she came with his pops he allowed her inside. As everyone sat around having drinks Marvin heard his door bell ring. He looked over at his surveillance camera, and saw The Terminator and what looked like two sercurity guards with him. "Let that Nigga in" Marvin yelled over his shoulder.

The Terminator stormed inside the house with a nervous look on his face, like he had just seen a ghost.

"What's up champ?" Marvin smiled looking The Terminator up and down. After just one glance he could tell that something wasn't right. "What's wrong with you?"

"That bitch Pauleena" The Terminator started off grabbing a bottle of water, and taking a swig. "The bitch came up to my gym with like fifteen of her henchmen flashing guns all over the place" he paused to take another sip of water. "Came up in there talking about I better take a dive in my next fight or else she's going to have me killed."

"Damn Nigga! You look shook" Moonie laughed.

"Nah this ain't no game, this bitch is for real" The Terminator told them. "She even shot one of my sparring partners"

"This shit is going too far" Romelo said as he sent Christie out into the sitting area so she couldn't hear anything that was being said.

"Fuck that bitch" Marvin downed his shot in one gulp. "I got too much money riding on this fight for you to take a dive."

"So what the fuck am I supposed to do if this crazy bitch storms into my gym again" The Terminator huffed.

"Calm down" Marvin stood up. "I'll have a few of my men hold you down."

"This shit ain't no joke" The Terminator continued his rant. "My mind needs to be clear while I'm training, or else nobody, won't be winning no money!"

"I'll take care of it" Marvin said looking over at Smitty. "Have a few of your best soldiers hold this Nigga down where ever he goes."

"This the biggest fight of my life" The Terminator reminded Marvin.

"I got you" Marvin said as he answered his ringing cell phone. "Yo who this?" He asked.

"Hey Marvin it's Nancy, sorry for calling you so late" she apologized.

"It's no problem. You know I don't sleep, what did I do to deserve a phone call from you?"

"I hate to bother you, but I kind of need a big favor" Nancy said.

"Anything you name it" Marvin sensed that something was wrong for her to be calling him so late.

"I don't really want to talk over the phone, is it possible that you can come over to my house please?"

Marvin flicked his wrist, glanced at his rolex that read 2:43am. "I'm on my way, I'll be there in twenty minutes" he said ending the call. "Come take a ride with me real quick" Marvin said as he, and Smitty stormed out the door.

* * *

Pauleena sat at her round table looking at her four main soldiers. Knowledge, Eraser Head, Roy and Paco, the five of them had been coming up with the perfect plan to get rid of Marvin, and his crew. Pauleena felt that Marvin wasn't on her level, and wanted to make an example out of him.

"Me, and a few of homies bumped into Marvin, and his whole army the other night" Knowledge said. "Dumped on them niggaz in they own hood" he boasted.

"Just because we at war, we still have to stay on the workers, and make sure the money keeps running in" Pauleena reminded everyone at the table. "Eraser Head, and Roy I want y'all to keep everybody on they job, anybody that owes us I need y'all to go out, and collect" she said watching Eraser Head, and Roy leave to go handle they business. "All I need you two to do is hold me down, and keep these niggaz up off my ass."

"That won't be a problem" Knowledge said with a smile. He lived to put in work, action excited him. Any chance he got to act a fool he took full advantage of it.

"I got a feeling them clowns are about to try to make a move on us, so be on point."

* * *

"I need a favor"

Nancy sat on her leather sofa, with an ice pack on her face. She couldn't believe Coco's new man Tony had put his hands on her. When his big hand connected with her it immediately brought back memories of when Dave used to beat her ass for no reason. Times like these were when she really needed to hear Ali's voice. Nancy pulled out her cell phone, and sent Ali a text that read. "Baby something bad just happened, I know you not speaking to me, but I really need to talk to you...pls." She knew Ali kept his cell phone on him at all times in jail, she just hoped he would give her a call or at least reply back to her text message. A loud knock at the front door startled Nancy, as she rushed over to the door, and opened it.

"What's up is everything alright?" Marvin asked stepping inside with his gun in hand followed by Smitty.

"No, everything is not alright" Nancy told him with tears streaming down her face. "I need a big favor from you."

"Name it" Marvin looked her in her eyes. Whoever had made Nancy cry was definitely going to have hell to pay.

"A friend of mines has this new boy friend" she sobbed. "And he just be beating her ass for no reason, I went over there to try and help her, and her boyfriend snapped, and started beating both of our asses."

"So the Nigga just snapped for no reason?" Smitty asked with a disbelieving look on his face. "Your friend had to do something."

"She didn't do anything" Nancy wiped her face dry. "Can ya'll help me?"

"You got an address?" Marvin asked smoothly.

"Yeah" Nancy answered in a weak voice. "I want you to kill that bastard."

The trio piled in the Yukon, heading towards Coco's house. The entire ride was filled with silence, each person caught up in their own thoughts. All Nancy cared about was seeing Tony get what he deserved. Twenty minutes later Smitty pulled up in front of Coco's house, and let the engine die.

"Stay here, we'll be right back" Marvin said as him, and Smitty hopped out the truck, and headed straight for the front door. Nancy watched from the back seat in shock when she saw Smitty kick open the front door. Marvin and Smitty quickly entered the house seconds later Nancy heard two loud shots go off.

"Oh my god" she said covering her mouth. When she told Marvin she wanted him to kill Tony, she didn't mean literally. Nancy quickly hopped out the truck, and headed towards the house to stop Marvin from committing murder.

Inside the house Tony sat on the couch with a cup of Henny in one hand, and the remote in the other. He was heading up stairs to beat Coco's ass again, just as soon as he finished with his drink. Coco's phone had rung at 3 AM, when she didn't answer it that made Tony think she had to hide from him, and for that Coco was going to have to pay. Just as Tony finished up his drink he saw the front door come crashing in. Tony eyes got big when he saw two men enter his house both holding pistols.

"What y'all think y'all doing?" Tony's questioning came to an end when he felt two bullets rip through both of his knee caps dropping him right where he stood. Marvin stood over Tony's body with his gun pointed right between the man's eyes.

"No don't kill him!" Nancy yelled finally making it inside the house happy that she had caught Marvin in time. "He's not even worth it."

Smitty ignored Nancy's comments as he kneeled down and began pistol whipping Tony. He didn't come all the way over here for nothing. Seconds later Coco finally came down stairs looking like she had just woke up. "What the fuck is going on down here?!"

"Baby, help me!" Tony begged with his face covered in blood.

"Nancy why did you bring these people to my house!?" Coco yelled as she ran and kneeled down by Tony's side. "Oh my God, baby are you alright?" Coco hopped up to her feet, and lunged towards Nancy, but Smitty caught Coco before she was able to reach Nancy.

"Bitch imma fuck you up when I catch you!" Coco growled with fire dancing in her eyes. She couldn't believe that Nancy would bring some strangers to her house to kill her boyfriend.

"I was just trying to help" Nancy said feeling bad.

"Well bitch thanks a lot" Coco said through clenched teeth.

"You silly bitch all she was trying to do was keep you from getting yo ass beat" Smitty shook his head at Coco's ignorance. He couldn't understand how some women could be so blind to the obvious.

"Sorry" Nancy said as her Marvin, and Smitty exited Coco's house.

"No bitch you gonna be sorry" Coco threatened as she slammed the door behind the trio.

"Damn all I was trying to do was help" Nancy said in a light whisper when they all was back in the truck.

"Your friend got issues" Marvin told her. "You can't help somebody that doesn't want to be helped."

"It has to be more to this, cause Coco's not the type to just let a Nigga be beating her ass" Nancy said out loud. For the rest of the ride every one was quiet. When Smitty finally pulled up in front of Nancy's house she sound asleep.

"We here baby" Marvin whispered shaking Nancy gently until she woke up. Marvin didn't know what Nancy had did to him, but for some reason he had to have her. "When can I see you again?" He asked placing his hand on her lower back, as they walked to front door.

"I've already told you I have a man" Nancy reminded him. "But I wouldn't mind going out for lunch some day."

Marvin smiled. He knew he was finally breaking her down. "That's what I'm talking about."

"But I have to pick the spot, cause the last time I was out with you, I almost got killed" she chuckled.

"Not a problem baby" Marvin leaned in, and kissed Nancy on the cheek.

"A'ight I'll see you soon" Nancy said stepping inside her house. She quickly slipped out of her clothes, and hopped in the bed. She kind of felt kind of bad for what had went down, but all she was doing was trying to help. Nancy really hoped that Coco didn't start acting stupid, cause she didn't want to have to beat her ass, but if she had to then she definitely would.

"Pay Up"

Loco sat in Monique's house at the kitchen table counting money, trying to tune her, and her nagging voice out. He was truly tired of Monique and her shit, but for the time being this was the only place he could stay rent free while he saved his money. Loco knew in two more months him, and Monique's relationship would be over, but until then he had to do what he had to do.

"I need some money" Monique said eyeing all the money that laid in a pile on the table.

"You just want some money, cause it's right in front of you" Loco huffed not falling for the bullshit.

"I need some new shoes!" Monique said like that was supposed to mean something. "And I need to go to the supermarket. We ain't got shit to eat."

"Food?" Loco repeated. "I thought you brought some food stamps from that chick with all those kids."

"Damn I gotta give you my life story just for you to give me a few dollars?" Monique scowled looking Loco up, and down. "You know what...fuck you, and your bullshit! I don't need this shit! Imma good muthafucking woman, got me begging you for some chump change!"

"Yo what is you talking about?" Loco stood to his feet.

"What I'm talking about!?" Monique echoed. "I'm supposed to be wifey, and you got me begging you for small change!"

"I just gave you $2,000 last week so you could go shopping" he reminded her.

"You talking like $2,000 is a lot of money" Monique said looking at Loco like he was insane. "You can't get shit nowadays with a crummy $2,000."

All Loco could do was look at Monique, and shake his head at how ignorant she was. Of course $2,000 was chump change especially when it wasn't coming from out of her pocket. Loco packed all his money up in a duffle bag, and then headed to the bedroom. He tossed the duffle bag in the closet, as he picked up his ringing cell phone. He looked at the caller ID and knew it was about to be a problem when he saw Eraser Head name flashing across the screen. Loco knew this day would come, when he had to break the news to Eraser Head and Pauleena that he wanted to do his own thing. "Yo what up?" He answered.

"Yo me, and Roy downstairs" Eraser Head told him. "Don't have us waiting long, and don't forget to bring that bread with you" he said ending the call.

Loco quickly dialed Gunplay's number as he grabbed his P89 off the dresser placing it in the small of his back. "Yo it's on meet me in front of my building in two minutes!" He slammed his phone shut, then headed out the door. Loco had too much real shit going on for him to be worried about what Monique was fussing about. Loco felt like his heart was about to beat out of his chest as he boarded the empty elevator. He quickly double checked the magazine to his P89 as he said a quick silent prayer before exiting the elevator. Loco stepped out the building, and immediately spotted Eraser Head, and Roy leaning up against a silver Range Rover. Young Jeezy's song "Rap Game" bumped through the speakers as the two men nodded their Head's to the beat.

The closer Loco got the more nervous he became. He had put in more than enough work in his day, but he'd never had an enemy as big as Pauleena would be. It was too late to turn back now. "What's good my niggaz?" He greeted the two men by giving them dap. Eraser Head looked at Loco like he was crazy, when he looked down, and didn't see him carrying any money.

"Where that bread at fam?" Eraser Head threw it out there not wasting no time. He was already in a bad mood, so today wasn't the day for excuses.

"Imma keep it real with you my Nigga" Loco began. "I ain't really feeling those numbers you and Pauleena threw at me. I feel like y'all holding me back from growing so I decided I was gon do my own thing" right on que Gunplay, Taz, and the rest of the crew surrounded the Range Rover.

"I don't give a fuck what you do" Eraser Head said looking Loco dead in his eyes. "Pauleena sent me here to collect, and that's what I'm going to do, so we can do this like civilized people, or this whole shit can turn ignorant real quick!"

"Tell Pauleena I said she dead on her money" Loco said pulling his gun from the small of his back. "Now y'all two chimps got thirty seconds to get the fuck up out my hood." Roy thought about making a move, but decided against it since he and Eraser Head was out manned and out gunned.

"We'll be back" Eraser Head smirked as he, and Roy hopped back in the Range Rover, and disappeared down the street. Loco watched as the Range Rover's tail lights disappeared down the street. He knew once Pauleena got word on what had went down shit was more than likely going to get ugly, but it was too late to change his decision now. "Let's get this money" he told his crew.

* * *

"WHAT YOU DOING?"

"Aye Hoe! You Know I Got That A1!" Rick Ross's voice boomed through the club's speaker, as the whole club chanted along. Moonie sat over in the corner on top of the table. In front of her were three different bottles of liquor. What started out as she, and Santana having a night all to themselves turned into Moonie sitting over at their V.I.P section all alone. Santana had told her he was going to the bathroom, but that was over thirty minutes ago. Moonie was trying her hardest to remain calm, but Santana was definitely testing her patience. She knew he was somewhere in the club fucking with some bitches. She could feel it in her stomach. "Fuck this shit!" Moonie huffed as she hopped up. She was tired of sitting at the table alone she was going to find her man. As Moonie snaked her way through the club, she felt several different men trying to grab her by her hand, she snatched her hand away each time as she continued on with her search. Moonie wore a white wife beater, up top, down low she wore a pair of pink Good2Go leggins, and a pair of white open toe 4 inch heels. Her weave was freshly done, and stopped at the middle of her back. Moonie squeezed through the club until she finally spotted Santana over by the bar all up in some light skin chick's face.

Moonie sighed loudly as she walked up and interrupted the two's conversation. "So this is what you over here doing while I'm sitting over there looking stupid waiting for you?" Santana went to reply, but Moonie snuffed him before the lie he was about to tell could leave his lips. Santana's head jerked back from the punch. "Fuck is wrong with you!?" He said through a pair of bloody lips.

"I don't know why I even started dealing with yo stupid young ass anyway!" Moonie looked him up and down like he was pathetic before she turned, and left him standing there with a busted lip looking stupid.

"Clown ass Nigga" Moonie said to herself as she headed back over to her table, right now she definitely needed a drink.

* * *

Knowledge and three of his henchmen entered the club with angry looks on their faces. Knowledge only hung out with niggaz that was fresh out of jail or either on their way to jail. He had got word that a few of Marvin's people's were supposed to be partying here tonight, some chick named Moonie, and some soft fake pretty boy who went by the name Santana. Knowledge had only seen a picture of the couple, but knew when he saw them up in person he would recognize them. He couldn't get his gun inside the club, so he settled for getting his homemade shank inside instead.

Young Chris's song "Racks On Racks" came blaring through the speakers, and the club went crazy. Knowledge squeezed through the crowded club looking at all the beautiful women who attended the party. The DJ had the party jumping when he scratched, and switched the song to Waka Flocka's "Grove Street Party!"

Knowledge tried to squeeze through a pack of women, when a caramel chick grabbed his jeans, and began grinding up him. He looked down and watched as the sexy chick did her thing. His crew quickly engaged with the rest of the women from Caramel's crew. After two songs had pasted Knowledge got Caramel's number, them brushed her off, and continued on with his search. After 30 minutes of searching through the big club Knowledge was starting to get frustrated, for a second he was starting to think that Moonie, and Santana wasn't in the club, or either had left already.

"We gon circle this bitch one more time, then we out" Knowledge told his henchmen.
* * *

Moonie sat over in the corner downing drink after drink. She was really contemplating on if she should kill Santana for trying to play her. If he just wanted sex with no strings attached, then he should of said that from the beginning instead of making Moonie think he was really feeling her. As Moonie sat at her table she couldn't stop her leg from shaking. She looked through the crowd, and saw Santana heading over towards her table. "If I stay here, imma wind up killing this mufucka!" Moonie said to herself standing to her feet, and heading for the exit. Moonie was in such a rush to get away from Santana that she accidentally bumped into a man spilling her drink all across his chest.

* * *

Knowledge and his henchmen stood in the middle of the dance floor, looking for their intended targets when some chick bumped into Knowledge stepping on his brand new Prada sneakers, and spilling a drink on his shirt. "Bitch!" Knowledge growled as he pushed the chick back into the crowd. "Watch where the fuck you going!"

Moonie went spilling back into the crowd. Once she caught her balance she jumped all up in man's face. "Put yo hands on me again, and I'll air this whole shit out!" She shouted pointing her finger all up in Knowledge's face. Knowledge looked down at the chick like she was crazy. Without even thinking twice he cocked back, and stole on Moonie knocking her out cold. When Knowledge looked down at the woman he realized she was the one he had been searching for all night. Just as Knowledge was about to pull out his shank, and finish Moonie off he noticed some big Diesil Nigga take his shirt off, and approach him.

"It's easy for you to knock a woman down" the diesel man said looking Knowledge up, and down. "Try doing that shit with someone your own size!"

Before Knowledge could even react one of his henchmen had already snuffed the big man. The other two henchmen quickly jumped into the fight turning it into a three on one. When Knowledge turned his attention back to Moonie he saw the pretty boy he had been looking for kneeling down next to Moonie.

"Get ya bitch ass up!" Knowledge yelled snatching Santana to his feet, with one hand, with the other he swiftly plunged his shank in, and out of Santana's neck repeatedly until the man's body finally dropped. Knowledge and his henchmen made a bee line for the exit once they saw Santana on the floor grabbing at his neck.

Outside Knowledge headed straight to his new Dodge Charger and hopped inside leaving the parking lot smelling like burnt rubber. He knew after this Marvin had no choice but to retaliate.

***

Pauleena's driver pulled up in front of The Terminator gym, and shifted the gear to park. "Keep this bitch running" Pauleena said as she, and Paco hopped out then entered the gym. Pauleena stepped foot in the gym, and heard Fabolous' new mix tape bumping from the speakers. After a few minutes of searching she finally spotted The Terminator working the heavy bag. Around him were several rough looking dudes posted up looking like they were supposed to be protecting him.

Pauleena smiled as she, and Paco approached The Terminator. Immediately they were met by the fake security.

"What's good?" One of the men asked with a mean look on his face.

"I need to speak to the champ" Pauleena replied.

"He's busy training right now...come back later" the man said in a dismissive tone. Paco took a step forward, but Pauleena's hand on his chest restrained him.

"Listen you stupid mufucka" Pauleena paused. "I'm going to give you three seconds to get the fuck out of my way" before things got out of hand. The Terminator stepped away from the punching bag to see what was going on. "What's the problem?" He asked breathing heavily.

"I just came to check on my investment" Pauleena smiled. She knew she had The Terminator right where she wanted him. Either he played by her rules, or suffer the consequences.

"Is there anything I can help you with? If not I have to get back to training" The Terminator spoke with confidence knowing he had Marvin's people's holding him down.

"Training?" Pauleena busted out laughing. "I don't think you understand, you are going to lose this fight or either you going to lose your life the choice is yours."

"I'm not sure I can do that" The Terminator held his ground. "I got a lot of people depending on me, and letting them down isn't a option" he knew he was taking a chance talking to Pauleena like that, but he also knew that she wouldn't harm him until after the fight.

"Like i said I dont think you understand" Pauleena grinned. "But I'll be sure to make sure you feel where I'm coming from."

The Terminator held a nervous look on his face, as he watched Pauleena, and the mystery man she came with exit his gym. He didn't know what to think, but what he did know was that she would definitely be back.

Outside Pauleena slid in the back seat of the Benz truck. She didn't really like how The Terminator was talking, and acting like he was willing to take his chances. She looked over at Paco, and gave him a quick head nod. Paco quickly popped open his suitcase that rested in the front seat, and removed his custom made Uzi. He placed a fresh clip in the base, cocked back the slide, and then headed back inside the gym.

The Terminator stood in front of the heavy throwing powerful left and right hooks when he noticed the man who was just with Pauleena re-enter the gym. Once The Terminator saw what the man was holding in his hands he, and his trainer jetted towards the back exit just as the gun shots rang out in the gym.

Paco entered the gym, and squeezed the trigger on the Uzi. He swayed his arms back, and forth hitting anything moving. He didn't take his finger off the trigger until there were no more bullets left inside the machine gun. Paco then quickly back peddled out of the gym, and into the back seat of the awaited ride. Pauleena smiled when she saw Paco slide in the back seat with her. At the moment she felt untouchable, she did what she wanted, when she wanted to, and she felt that there was no one who could stop her or her movement.

"You need to let me find those clowns leader so i can put an end to this" Paco said gently placing his Uzi back in its suitcase.

"Marvin's been hiding like a little bitch lately" Pauleena told him. "But once he begins to show his face again, I'll make sure it gets blown off." Once Marvin was out of the way Pauleena planned on taking a much needed vacation, just to get away for a while.

Back at her mansion Pauleena, and Paco sat at the bar having drinks, while seven of her Muslim security guards roamed the property looking out for any signs of trouble.

"I thank you for the opportunity" Paco downed his drink in one gulp. "I needed to get away, and I could definitely use the money."

"Why, wassup?" Pauleena asked refilling both of their glasses. She knew Paco made good money killing so to hear he needed the money was kind of a shocked to her.

"Back home I fucked around, and killed a very important man" Paco said in a light whisper. "Now I have to get up 3 million dollar to give to the man's family or else they gonna have me killed."

"Why the fuck didn't you tell me about this sooner!" Pauleena yelled. "We family I would have given you the money."

"You know I don't work like that" he reminded her. "I've never been the one to take a hand out."

"A handout?" Pauleena repeated. "These people will kill you, and think nothing of it!"

"I know" Paco said downing another shot. "Whenever I do go, better believe I'm going out with a bang" he smiled.

Pauleena poured them both another shot when she noticed a lot of movement in her survailance monitors. "What the fuck?" She said with a confused look on her face as she watched several cop cars swarm the front of her house. "Look at these pussies" she tapped Paco to get his attention.

"We banging out?" Paco asked ready for whatever. Jail was a place where he couldn't see himself being, he'd rather be dead, then locked in a cage.

"No let's see how this plays out first" Pauleena smiled. "If anything we'll be out by the morning."

Two of Pauleena Muslim security guards came running in. "The cops are here what you want us to do?" He asked with a pistol in each hand.

"Stand down" Pauleena announced to her whole team. The last thing she wanted right now was a shootout with the police. Seconds later the police busted the door open with a battery ram, and in ran what looked to be about fifty to sixy officers. "GET ON THE GROUND!" They all yelled at once.

"I'm not doing shit until I see a warrant" Pauleena said finishing off her drink.

"Well, well, well" Detective Nelson sang as he entered the mansion with a piece of paper in his hand. His hard bottom shoes clacked loudly against the marble floor. "Pauleena I've heard so much about you" he said standing directly in front of her. In a swift motion Detective Nelson pulled out his .357 and back slapped Paco across the face with it knocking him out cold. "Eyeball me again!" He yelled looking down at Paco's unconscious body.

Detective Nelson slid his weapon back down into his holster and then gave Pauleena his undivided attention. "Word on the streets is you've been making a lot of money out here on the streets" he smiled. "I want in."

"I don't know what you talking about" Pauleena replied. "You must got me mixed up with somebody else."

"Oh really" Detective Nelson smirked as he punched Pauleena in her stomach causing her to drop down to her knees. "I'm not the one you want to fuck with" he grabbed her by her hair forcing her to look at him. "You will break me off 15% of what you are bringing in or I'll make your life a living hell!" He tossed Pauleena back down to the floor, and shoved his knee down on her neck as he cuffed her, and began searching the large house. An hour later sixteen guns were found throughout the property.

"Why do you have sixteen guns in your home?" Detective Nelson asked with his famous grin on his face.

"Lawyer" Pauleena replied in a bored tone. She knew the detective was just fishing for information. "You must not know who I am."

"I don't give a fuck!" Detective Nelson turned and back slapped Pauleena across her face like she was a random whore. He then roughly shoved her in the back seat. "After spending a few nights in jail, maybe you'll see that in my world you are powerless" he said slamming the back door shut. Pauleena didn't know who this detective was, but one thing she knew was he wouldn't be breathing for much longer.

"SERIOUS BUSINESS"

Eraser Head and Knowledge sat staked out across the streets from the projects. For the past two days they'd been scoping out the projects looking for Loco and any of the main members of his crew. Two days had passed, and still no sign of Loco.

"I'm not with this cat, and Mouse shit!" Knowledge spat. "I say we go to his crib, and make his bitch talk."

"Let's just chill for another hour, and see if this clown shows" Eraser Head suggested. Knowledge sighed loudly. He didn't like how Eraser Head handled things. He felt that the man was soft, and scared to take things to the next level. Knowledge still couldn't understand how Eraser Head had become the next in charge. He didn't have enough to be in charge. As the two men sat in the car, Knowledge spotted Loco's girlfriend getting out of cab with a lot of bags in her hand.

"There go his bitch right there" Knowledge pointed out. "I say we go make her talk."

"Chill let's wait it out, I got a feeling this clown is gon show up any minute" Eraser Head said.

"Fuck this waiting shit!" Knowledge huffed stepping out of the car. He was tired of just sitting around waiting for something to happen. It was time for him to make something happen. He followed Monique into the building, and quickly held the door for pretending to be the perfect gentleman.

"Thank you" Monique said happy she was finally home. She had been out shopping all day, and couldn't wait to get upstairs so she could get off her feet. Monique and Knowledge hopped on the elevator together. Once the elevator door closed Knowledge pulled out his .40 Cal and aimed it at Monique's head.

"Where the fuck is that nigga Loco at!?" He growled. Monique looked down the barrel of the gun, and almost shitted on herself. Loco hadn't been home in the past week, and now she figured out why.

"I haven't seen him in a week, I swear to God" Monique said with her eyes closed.

"Bitch you better not be lying!" Knowledge huffed grabbing Monique by the back of her neck roughly escorting her out of the elevator. Monique's heels stabbed the floor with each step she took until she finally reached her front door. She stuck her key in the lock, and quickly opened the door. Once the door was open Knowledge shoved her inside the apartment as he slammed, and locked the door behind him.

"Please don't kill me" Monique begged.

"Where's the stash?" Knowledge said looking around. He knew Loco had to have left some money with his girl.

"What stash?" Monique replied with a nervous look on her face.

"Bitch don't play stupid with me" Knowledge warned. "All this mufucking shopping you doing, it must be some money up in here somewhere."

"Ain't no money up in here" Monique announced. "Loco don't give a fuck about me, why you think he just left me for dead like this?"

Knowledge aimed his gun at Monique's head, and pulled the trigger without hesitation. Once that was done Knowledge ransacked the apartment, searching for anything valuable. After a ten minute search Knowledge returned to the living room, and shot Monique again, mad cause he didn't find anything in the apartment.

Knowledge walked from the building back to the car with an angry look on his face. He had his mind fixed on finding a stash inside the apartment.

"How did it go?" Eraser Head asked once Knowledge slid back inside the car. From the look on his face he knew it had went bad.

"I put in that work" Knowledge boasted.

"And what did that accomplish?" Eraser Head asked pulling away from the scene.

"A lot" Knowledge answered quickly. "For starters it sends a clear message that we ain't fucking around!"

Eraser Head chuckled. "Fam we in this business to make money, how did what you did help to get the money that Loco still owes us?"

"Listen you punk mufucka" Knowledge huffed. "If you was out here handling shit the way it's supposed to getting handled...then I wouldn't have to come, and clean up your mess!"

"You right" Eraser Head said just to end the conversation. He refused to go back and forth with an ignorant idiot like Knowledge. With the way Knowledge was going, he would either be dead or in jail soon Eraser Head said to himself, as he dropped Knowledge off at some stripper's crib.

Eraser Head knew if he didn't get rid of Knowledge soon, he would definitely sink the whole operation with his cowboy antics. Eraser Head had too many people depending on him to just sit back, and let that happen.
***

"Visiting Hours"

Ali sat in his cell doing mad push ups. Ever since Crystal had been tossed off the top tier by Big Blood, Ali had been staying to himself. He worked out all day to try and keep his mind off all the shit that was going on in his life. The warden had transferred Big Blood to another facility, so there was no way Ali could even get his revenge on the gang member. Ali hopped up off the floor, and splashed some water on his face knowing he had to spend the rest of his life in prison was finally starting to take a toll on him, no matter what happened he'd have to spend the rest of his life in a cell being told what to do, and when to do it. Ali flopped down on his bed, and grabbed all the unread letters he had received from Nancy. He never opened, or read her letters. Ali knew if had read any of the letters, he would of more than likely responded. Besides the word on the streets was, Nancy was now Marvin's woman. Ali had to smack the shit out of two guys who he over heard spreading the rumors. Just as Ali was about to make himself some crackhead soup, a C.O. walked up to his cell.

"Hey Ali you have a visitor" the C.O. Told him.

"A visitor?" Ali echoed with a confused look on his face. "Whoever it is I don't want to them."

"This is the fifth visit you've refused" the C.O. reminded him. "It might be an emergency."

"I don't want no visitors right now" Ali told him as he popped his Jim Jones tape in his walk man, and threw his head phones on. Whoever was here to see, he wanted nothing to do with them.

***

Nancy sat in the visiting room praying that this time Ali would accept her visit. She really needed to see, and speak to him. A lot of shit had been going on, and she really needed to speak to her other half. Nancy nervously tapped her finger nail on the table as two C.O.'s walked up to her.

"Ma'am Ali said he doesn't want any visitors today" the white officer said coldly.

"No, no, no" Nancy stood to her feet. "I'm not going anywhere until I see him" she was tired of this shit! She wasn't going anywhere until she saw her man.

"Ma'am!" The white officer said with authority. "I'm going to have to ask you to leave the facility, if not I'm going to have to lock you up."

"I don't give a fuck, do what you gotta do!" Nancy replied not backing down from the C.O.

The white officer quickly rushed Nancy tackling her down to the floor right in the middle of the visitor's room making a big scene. Nancy screamed loudly, kicking her feet wildly trying to break free the two C.O.'s who tried to restrain her.

"Get the fuck off me!!" Nancy screamed as the C.O.'s hand cuffed her, and carried her off to a holding room. "Get me the fuck outta here!" She yelled as the officers shut the door leaving her in there by herself. Nancy paced the room back and forth with her hands still cuffed behind her back. She didn't know what was going on, but what she did know was she wasn't going anywhere until she saw her man. Forty five minutes later the Nancy heard the door open, and in walked the Warden with three C.O.'s behind him.

"What seems to be the problem?" The warden asked with a lot of concern in his voice.

"I'm here to see my man Ali, and I'm not leaving until I do" Nancy told him. "It's been months since I've seen him or heard from him, and I'm not going anywhere until I see him!"

"Ma'am if you don't leave the facility, I'll be forced to lock you up" the warden said.

"Oh motherfucking well" Nancy sang. She was tired of all this bullshit. If she had to go to jail, then so be it.

"Let me see what I can do for you" the warden said as he turned exiting the room.

* * *

Ali sat in his cell sipping on some tang, flipping through the pages of a new magazine, from the corner of his eye he saw several people standing in front of his cell, when he looked up he saw the warden, and three C.O.'s standing there.

"What's the problem?" Ali asked taking his head phones off. The warden stepped Inside of Ali's cell, and sat down on his bed. "Let me have a word with him alone please" he ordered.

Once the guards left the warden began. "What's been going on with you?" he asked. "I've heard you ain't been out of your cell in weeks."

"I just been chilling, staying to myself trying to stay out of trouble" Ali told him.

"It's a beautiful woman here to see you" the warden told him. "Why do you keep on refusing her visit?"

"I can't worry about what's going on in the outside world, if I do that shit will drive me crazy" Ali sighed. "I love my woman, but I can't stand for her to see me like this."

"I understand" the warden said. "But Nancy is down in the visiting room, and she really wants to see you, she seems like a really lovely lady."

"That's my baby, but I just can't stand for her to see me like this" Ali repeated.

"She said she's not going anywhere until she see's you. If you don't go down, and see her, my men will have to lock her up, cause she's refusing to leave" the warden told him.

Ali sighed loudly. "I'll be down there in fifteen minutes"

"Thanks" The warden said as he got up, and exited the cell. Ali quickly got dressed, and headed down towards the visiting room. He was a little nervous about seeing Nancy since he hadn't seen her in a while. When Ali reached the visiting room all eyes were on him since everyone seen his girl get escorted out the visiting room kicking, and screaming. Ali sat down at an empty table. Minutes later, two C.O.'s escorted Nancy back into the visiting room. Nancy ran, and jumped in Ali's arms bear hugging him.

"Baby I missed you so much!" Nancy cried openly not caring who saw her. She was just happy to be in her man's arms.

"I missed you too baby" Ali whispered in her ear. It felt good to be holding his woman again, it seemed like it had been years since the two had seen each other. "How have you been?" Ali asked as the two sat down.

"Not good" Nancy huffed. "Why haven't you been responding to my letters, and denying my visits?"

"Baby it's hard enough with me being in here, I hate to have to see you come up here, and the look on your face when it's time to leave crushes my insides" Ali explained.

"And it crushes me when you shut me out like this" Nancy countered. "We supposed to be a team."

"We were I team."

"What you mean we were a team?" Nancy face crumbled up at the sound of that.

"Word on the streets is" Ali paused. "Is that you on Marvin's team now!"

"Marvin's team?" Nancy said confused. She wondered how he found out about them two while locked up. She had a feeling that's why he'd been shutting her, but wasn't really sure. She could only imagine the story he'd heard about her, and Marvin. "Who told you that?"

"It doesn't matter, just know I know everything that's going on."

"Me, and Marvin are just friends" Nancy explained. "We've never been on a date or nothing like that, I swear to you it's nothing like that, you know I would never cheat on you or disrespect you like that."

"You sure about that?" Ali asked inside his blood was boiling. He didn't care if Nancy wasn't fucking Marvin he didn't want her around another man period.

"Yes I'm sure" Nancy answered quickly. "Ever since you made me your queen, I've carried myself like nothing less."

"How you think it makes me feel to have to hear that my wife is out hanging out with the next up coming Nigga in the drug game?" Ali asked.

"I swear I will never talk to him ever again."

"Shouldn't of been talking to him from the beginning" Ali huffed. The shit Nancy was saying sounded kind of suspect, but for some reason he believed, and trusted that she wouldn't lie to him. As the two spoke Ali notice a small bruise by Nancy's eye that she clearly tried to cover with make up. "What happened to your face?"

Nancy shook her head as she told Ali the whole story about how Coco's man was putting his foot in her ass, and how the only person could help her was Marvin. She told him the whole story not leaving out any parts. It hurted Ali just knowing that it was nothing he could do if ever Nancy was in trouble.

"Can you please promise before I leave that you will keep all lines of communication open with me?" Nancy asked.

"I got you baby" Ali leaned over and passionately kissed Nancy, the two hugged for at least two minutes straight before the C.O. announced that visiting hours were over.

"Please call me tonight" Nancy said in a whining voice.

"I will" Ali said as he leaned in closer to Nancy's ear. "I don't want you hanging around Marvin no more you hear me?"

"Yes daddy I promise I'm done with that" Nancy promised as she slowly walked to the exit. Ali watched as Nancy exited the visiting room. Seeing her made him feel so much better, she always seemed to lift his spirit. Ali went back to his cell with a smile on his face, when he reached his cell Ali laid across his bed, and began reading all of Nancy's letters.

* * *

"WHAT'S POPPIN?"

After what had happened to Moonie and Santana at the club Marvin knew he had to do something quick, before the streets began to think he and his crew was weak. He'd heard about some new crazy mufucka named Paco who worked for Pauleena. Some how one of Marvin's people's had got the address to where Paco rested his head, and now it was time for Marvin and his crew to pay the so called crazy man a visit.

Smitty was behind the wheel of a raggedy van full with gunmen ready to shoot, and ask questions later. "You a'ight?" He asked looking over at Marvin in the passenger seat.

"I'm tired of this bitch Pauleena" Marvin said in a calm tone. "Whoever we find in this house I want them dead" there wasn't enough room on the streets for the two so someone had to go Marvin thought as the van pulled up to the front of the address the navigation had taken them too. Marvin looked out the window at the expensive house, and knew they had arrived at the right house. "Let's do this shit" Marvin said as he and his crew hopped out the van with their faces covered by a ski mask. One of Marvin's heavy set gunmen lifted his leg, and came forward with a strong kick against the front door kicking it open. Marvin watched as all his gunmen file inside the house one by one. He was the last to enter.

* * *

Paco stepped out the shower, quickly dried off, and wrapped his towel around his waist. He and Pauleena had just been released from jail a few hours. The only thing on Paco's mind right now was getting his hands on Detective Nelson. He hadn't been able to sleep since the punk ass detective had assaulted him. For that the detective would surely have to pay. As Paco stood looking at his reflection in the mirror, he heard a loud bang come from downstairs followed by footsteps. He quickly ran over to his gun closet, and snatched the doors open. Paco grabbed an M-16 that was hooked up with a flashlight and a few other things attached to it. Paco walked to the top of the steps, aimed the M-16 at the mask men, and pulled the trigger flooding the entire house with loud gunfire.

Marvin quickly took cover behind a wall, as bullets flew from all angles. He watched his soldiers return fire with the crazy man.

Paco jotted down the steps with his M-16 in his hand in the process his towel fell from his waist leaving his nude body exposed. "This what y'all wanted!?" He yelled squeezing the trigger again. Paco smiled as he watched all the mask men scramble for their lives.

Marvin sprung from behind the corner popping shot after shot with his Tech-9. Before taking cover back behind the wall. Smitty tried to dash through the kitchen to escape the gunfire, but was dropped dead in his tracks by one of Paco's M-16 bullets. Marvin watched as all of his gunmen dropped one by one. Marvin quickly sprung from behind the wall again this time he back peddled towards the front door recklessly sending shots in the crazy man's direction. Once he made it outside Marvin ran full speed towards the van, and hopped in the driver's seat. Every man he had come here with was now dead. Marvin started the van, and just as he was about to pull off he saw the crazy gunman come running out the house butt naked.

Paco ran outside butt naked and bare foot as he chased the van down the street riddling it with bullets until it finally bent the corner.

Marvin bent the corner happy that the gunman had finally stopped chasing the van. When he ran up in the house he didn't expect for things to get that wild, and out of hand. As he drove down the street he noticed people staring at the bullet filled van. "Fuck" Marvin cursed as he pulled over, snatched his ski mask off his face, and exit the van. He jogged down the street on foot hoping that no cops stopped him for look suspicious. When Marvin finally figured out where he was. He realized that Nancy's house was only a few blocks away. That's where he was headed until the heat died down.

* * *

Nancy stood over the sink washing dishes, every since her visit with Ali her spirit been on an all time high. She never knew how much she could love another person until she met Ali. Now that everything between Nancy, and Ali was back on good terms, she couldn't get rid of the smile that was splattered on her face. Drake's song "I'm on one" hummed softly through the speakers as Nancy answered her cell phone, as she poured herself a glass of red wine. "Hello" she answered.

"What's up baby" Ali said on the other line. He could hear Nancy smiling through the phone. Ali was also happy that the two was back on speaking terms. He had really missed talking to his other half.

"I'm just chilling right now having a drink" Nancy smiled. "How's Skip been holding up in there?"

"He's good. He'll finally be getting out at the end of the month."

"It's about time, I'm happy for him" Nancy said as she heard a loud knock at her front door.

"Fuck is that knocking on your door at this time of night?" Ali asked his jealous instincts kicking in immediately.

"I don't know baby" Nancy said nervously as she walked up to the door, and looked through the peek hole. Her heart dropped down to her stomach, when she saw Marvin standing on the other side of the door.

"Who the fuck is that at the door?" Ali asked again.

"It's Marvin" Nancy answered honestly. Once the words left her lips she knew she had made a mistake.

"Damn" Ali began feeling stupid. "So this Nigga can just pop up at our house at all times of the night, he got it like that?"

"No Ali it's not like that" Nancy tried to explain, as other knock echoed off the door. KNOCK! KNOCK! KNOCK! Nancy quickly opened the door. "Hey wassup" she asked nervously with Ali still on the phone. "You can't just be coming over....."

"I need to stay here for a second" Marvin cut her off, stepping inside the house. "The cops are looking for me. I promise I won't be here for long."

Nancy was stuck in an awkward situation. On one hand she didn't want Ali to be mad at her, and on the other she didn't want to see Marvin get locked up.

"Can I stay here for an hour or two?" Marvin asked standing in the middle of the living room. Nancy put one finger up to lips signaling Marvin to be quiet. "Hello, baby?....hello?" Nancy looked at her phone, and realized Ali had hung up. Right then, and there she knew that her, and Ali's relationship was more than likely over. If the tables were turned, and Nancy was in jail, and had heard a woman banging on her man's door in the middle of the night she probably would of reacted the same way.

"You a'ight?" Marvin asked sensing something was wrong. Nancy broke down in tears right in front of Marvin. It was a strong possibility that she just lost the best thing that ever happened to her.

"No I'm not alright" she cried. "You just costed me my relationship by barging over here like that!"

"What you mean?" Marvin said confused. He knew that nothing was going on between them, but he didn't think it would be a big deal that he went over there to lay low for a minute. "How did I cost you your relationship?"

"I was on the phone with Ali when you came banging on the door like the police" she said with much attitude. "Now he thinks me and you fucking."

"Why would he think that?"

Nancy sighed loudly. "Do you see what time it is?"

"Sorry baby" Marvin apologized.

"I'm not your baby!" Nancy snapped. Marvin looked at her for a second, right then, and there he knew she loved Ali with all of her heart. "Sorry for costing you all this trouble, I promise not to bother you again" Marvin said heading towards the door. As he walked towards the door he saw several infrared beams blared through the window. Marvin quickly ran towards Nancy, and tackled her down to the floor. "Get down!" He yelled as the two hit the floor, as the sounds of broken glass, and automatic assault rifles echoed throughout the house. Broken glass showered on top of Marvin, and Nancy's head. Once the gunfire paused Marvin quickly shot to his feet, and pulled his P89 from the small of his back, as he grabbed Nancy's hand leading her towards the back door. "We gotta get out of here!" He yelled.

"No wait!" Nancy yelled stopping in mid-stride snatching her hand away from his. "My son is upstairs sleeping in his room, I can't leave him" Nancy said as she quickly ran up stairs to Lil Ali's room. Marvin stood in the kitchen waiting for Nancy to return, when the front door got kicked in. BOOM!! Marvin put a bullet in the chest of the first two men through the door. He tried to keep the gunmen at bay until Nancy returned from upstairs, but there were just too many of them. One after other flooded Nancy's living room. "Shit!" Marvin cursed as he dodged bullets escaping out the back door. He felt bad about leaving Nancy alone in the house with a bunch of heartless killers, but he had to do what he had to do.

Once all the gun fire had ended, Pauleena stepped inside the house with a 9mm in her hand. She stepped on the broken glass until she stood in the middle of the living room where a few of her gunmen held Nancy and Lil Ali. Nancy rested on her knees in the middle of the floor held at gun point.

"Where did Marvin run to?" Pauleena asked in an even tone.

"I don't know" Nancy answered looking at the gun Pauleena held down by her side.

"You willing to die, to protect a Nigga that just left you and your son here for dead?" Pauleena said loading a round into the chamber.

"I swear I don't know where he went" Nancy cried. Seconds later Knowledge walked inside the house with one of his gunmen.

"I just finished chasing that bitch ass Nigga Marvin" Knowledge said out of breath. "That's a fast mufucka."

When Nancy saw Knowledge her eyes got wide, she didn't know him that well, but had seen him around Ali, and G-Money before her, and Ali had got locked up. "Please don't let her do this" Nancy begged looking in Knowledge's eyes.

"Yo what you doing?" Knowledge asked looking over at Pauleena. "This is Ali's wife."

"So what the fuck was Marvin doing over here at 2am?" Pauleena questioned. "We'd been following Marvin for days now, and he was a regular over here" she said looking down at Nancy.

"If she doesn't tell me where Marvin went, I'm going to have to kill her."

"I swear I don't know where he ran off too" Nancy said as warm tears streamed down her face.

"Please" Knowledge said looking down at Nancy. "If you want me to help you, you have to tell me where Marvin went. This has nothing to do with you, all we want is Marvin."

"I swear to God I don't know where he went or where he's going" Nancy confessed.

"She doesn't know where this chump is at" Knowledge said looking at Pauleena. "I know her, the only person she would ever protect like this Ali."

"Well I think the bitch is lying" Pauleena said never taking her eyes off of Nancy. She quickly reached down, and snatched Lil Ali from Nancy's arms. Nancy hung on to her son for dear life, but two of Pauleena's Muslim guards smoothly pried her hands off of the Lil boy.

"No please don't hurt my son he's just a child" Nancy begged like she'd never begged before.

"You better stop fucking around" Pauleena said looking down at Nancy. "I'm going to ask you one more time" she paused. "Where the fuck is Marvin?" She said pressing the barrel of her 9mm to Lil Ali's head.

"I swear to God I DO NOT KNOW!" Nancy pleaded.

Pauleena smirked. "You know what? I believe you."

Just as Nancy felt relieved she heard a single gun shot, and watched as Lil Ali's lifeless body fell to the floor in what seemed like slow motion. "Noooooooooo!" she screamed quickly crawling over to where Lil Ali's laid. "Wake up baby please wake up..."Nancy whispered. At the moment shit didn't even feel real. It took a minute for everything to register in Nancy's brain, when it finally did she jumped up, and lunged at Pauleena. One of the Muslim body guards quickly caught Nancy before she could reach Pauleena.

"I'm going to kill you bitch!" Nancy yelled inches away from Pauleena's face. "I swear to God you a dead bitch walking!!"

"Fuck you think you talking too?" Pauleena smiled aiming the 9mm at Nancy's head. "Say it again" she dared her. Nancy looked her in the eyes. "Bitch I'm going to kill you!"

Knowledge quickly stepped in the middle of the two women. "That's enough" he said looking at Pauleena.

"Ali's going to have you swimming with the fishes for just standing by letting this go on" Nancy said to Knowledge as she started laughing hysterically. "Both of y'all just got in over y'alls head"

Knowledge felt bad about what had just happened. If he could of stopped it he would of, he ignored Nancy's comments cause he knew Ali was never getting out of jail. When Knowledge was working with Ali, and G-Money he was loyal to them, now he was working with Pauleena, and he planned on being loyal to her as well.

"Tie this piece of trash up" Pauleena said nodding towards Nancy. "I bet Marvin comes to her rescue" she laughed.

"What if he doesn't?" Knowledge asked.

"If he doesn't come try to rescue this bitch in a week, then I'll personally kill her myself" Pauleena said exiting the house.

"Come on get her out of here" Knowledge ordered as he watched the rest of the gunmen tie Nancy up and escort her out the house.

"Knowledge please don't just leave my son here like that" Nancy begged. "You owe Ali at least that much."

"What you want me to do take him with me?" Knowledge asked.

"Let me call my girlfriend please I won't tell her what happened I swear, I'll just ask her to please come over here" Nancy said as she heard her cell phone ringing. She knew it was Ali from the ring tone she had assigned to him. "Can I answer that please?"

"No" Knowledge said quickly dismissing the question. He pulled out his cell phone. "What's your homegirl's phone number?" He punched in the number, and put the call on speaker phone. The phone rung five times before Coco finally answered. "Who this?"

"Coco it's me Nancy"

"Bitch didn't I tell you not to call my phone no more!?" Coco said as if Nancy was an annoyance. She was still mad about what had happen to her boyfriend Tony, in her mind it was all Nancy's fault.

"No Coco please don't hang up" Nancy begged. "I need you right now please."

Coco could hear the seriousness in Nancy's voice. She also heard that her former best friend was crying. "Me, and you have nothing to talk about, so I'll appreciate it if you didn't call me any more!"

"I need you to come over to my house please it's an emergency, if not for me please do it for your godson" Nancy said as Knowledge pressed the end button on the phone disconnecting the call. As Pauleena's Muslim body guards carried Nancy out of the house she said a silent prayer that Coco would find it in her heart to come to house.

***

"Who was that on the phone?" Tony asked when Coco hung up. Every since Marvin had whipped his ass, he'd had a new attitude, and started treating Coco the way she was supposed to be treated. Sometimes a good ass whipping would do that to you.

"That was Nancy" Coco sucked her teeth. "After what that bitch did she got a lot of nerves calling me talking about she need me to go over there."

Tony didn't like Nancy, but he knew deep down inside Coco had missed talking, and spending time with her best friend. He kind of felt bad for keeping Coco hostage in the house, he knew she was faithful, and loyal to him. "Why don't you go make up with your friend, and see if she's alright."

"Fuck that bitch" Coco huffed. "After what she did to us...I wish I would."

"Everything I got, I more than deserved" Tony told her. "A friendship like y'all's only come around once in a lifetime."

Coco sighed loudly as she stood to her feet. "I'm only doing this for you." She said to Tony before she stormed out the house. Coco didn't want to see Nancy, but from the tone of her voice she could tell that it had to be something serious. Thirty minutes later Coco pulled up to Nancy's house with an attitude, but when she saw the front door wide open she knew something bad had went down inside the house. Coco hopped out her Lexus, and ran as fast as she could in her heels. When Coco stepped inside the house immediately she threw up at the site of Lil Ali's dead body. She couldn't believe what her eyes were seeing. Coco quickly pulled out her cell phone, and dialed 911. When Coco got off the phone with the police she heard Nancy's cell phone ringing. She slowly walked over to the phone not sure if she should answer it or not. Coco looked at the caller ID. On the cell phone, she immediately answered it when she saw Ali's name flashing across the screen. "Oh my god Ali I don't know what the fuck is going! I just got here, and Lil Ali is dead!" She said in a vast pitched voice.

"Hold on, hold on, slow down I can't understand shit you saying" Ali said sitting up in his bunk.

"Nancy called me crying begging me to come over, when I got here I saw somebody shot the whole house up, when I stepped inside I saw Lil Ali laying on the floor dead! The whole house is fucked up, and it's no sign of Nancy anywhere!" she told him.

Ali couldn't believe what he was hearing, in his mind he thought he was dreaming, but the sad part was he knew he was wide awake. "Are you telling me my son is dead?" He asked just to make sure he was hearing right.

"Yes I just called 911" Coco cried. "I hope Nancy is okay."

Ali didn't have anything else to say so he just hung up, and cried his eyes out for the rest of the night. Ali felt powerless in jail, he knew if he was home none of this shit would of never happened, so he blamed himself for everything that happened. While all this was going on all he could do was sit, and rot in jail.

"REMEMBER ME"

Detective Nelson pulled up in front of his house with a frown on his face. He was pissed because neither Marvin nor Pauleena seemed to be falling into his trap. Detective Nelson was missing out on the street money that he was used to making with Ali, and Rell. Now that his well had dried up he was in desperate need of some quick money. "Fuck this shit" Detective Nelson huffed stepping out his car. He was just going to have to come down harder on Marvin and Pauleena's crews until one of them finally broke. Detective Nelson walked up to his run down apartment when out of nowhere a gloved hand covered his mouth as he felt some cold steel being pressed to the side of his head.

"I dare you to scream" Paco whispered in Detective Nelson's ear as he forcefully shoved him inside the apartment.

"I wouldn't do this is I was you" Detective Nelson said trying to talk his way out of the sticky situation. "I'm a very important man. If I come up missing...it's going to get real ugly for you."

Seconds later Pauleena stepped inside the apartment with one of her Muslim body guards in tow. "Nice to see you again detective" she said with a smirk on her face. "Restrain this cocksucker" she ordered. The Muslim body guard smoothly punched Detective Nelson in his stomach causing him to drop to one knee doubled over in pain. The body guard then hand cuffed Detective Nelson with his own cuffs.

"Didn't I tell you, you were fucking with the wrong one?" Pauleena said as she removed the jacket to her thousand dollar grey suit she wore. Just the site of the defenseless cop standing before Pauleena brought a smile to her face. She rolled up her sleeves before smacking the shit out of Detective Nelson. "So you like throwing your weight around, and steal from hard working hustlers?" Pauleena said sarcastically as her fist connected with the detective's face again. "Imma show you how a mufucka throw they weight around" Pauleena nodded at her Muslim body guard. The body guard slowly walked up to Detective Nelson, and went to work on him. Pauleena and Paco sat back, and laughed as they watched Detective Nelson's head snap back and forth from each powerful blow that the Muslim guard delivered. After the two got tired, of watching the detective take a beating Pauleena stepped in. "I got $5,000 say one of my bullets can kill him, before yours can."

"That's a bet" Paco smiled. "Ladies first"

Pauleena stepped up, removed one of her 9mm from her shoulder holster, aimed it at Detective Nelson's chest, and pulled the trigger. POW!

Next Paco stepped up, and fired a shot in Detective Nelson's stomach. The two took turns firing shots at Detective Nelson's body until he finally died.

"Cocksucker!" Pauleena huffed pressing her 9mm against Detective Nelson's head. She pulled the trigger splattering his brains all over the floor, and wall as she, Paco, and her body guard exited the apartment.

"PAIN IS LOVE"

Ali lay on his bunk staring at the latest picture he had of Lil Ali. He couldn't believe that somebody had murdered his son, and kidnapped his fiancé. Murderous thoughts flowed through his mind the more he thought about the whole situation. Someone tapping on Ali's cell caused him to sit up.

Skip stood by Ali's cell with his bag by his feet. Today was the day he was finally being released back into society. "How you holding up in there?"

"I'll live" Ali said dryly. He was sad about Lil Ali, but he was happy that Skip was finally getting released today.

"Soon as I hit the streets imma find out who did this to Lil Ali, and handle that shit for you" Skip said confidently.

"Nah" Ali said quickly." April been by your side for these past five years patiently waiting for you to get out, don't break that girls heart, by doing some dumb shit thats gon land you right back in here.....what's done is done" Ali told him, as the two hugged for about two minutes. "You make sure you take care of your wife, this streets shit is over you hear me?"

Skip nodded his head as a tear escaped his eye. "If you ever need anything, and I mean anything just name it."

"You already know" Ali smiled as he watched a C.O. escort Skip down the tier, and out of the jail. Just as Ali went to lay back down a C.O. arrived at his cell notifying him that he had a visitor here to see him. At first Ali thought about denying the visit, but thought it might of been Nancy. Ali quickly threw his state green shirt on, and followed the C.O. down to the visiting room. When he reached the visiting room he didn't see Nancy nowhere in site. As he stood looking around he noticed a man sitting alone at a table waving him over. Ali walked over to the table to see what the man wanted.

"Hey Ali wassup I'm Marvin" Marvin said motioning for Ali to have a seat.

"You got a lot of balls coming up here" Ali said through clenched teeth.

"Listen I didn't come here for all that" Marvin huffed. "I know who took Nancy."

"Who?"

"Some chick named Pauleena" Marvin told him. "It's all my fault they were gunning for me, and I happened to be at her house, but fuck all that I gotta get her back."

"You gotta get her back?" Ali repeated. "Nigga it's your fault that my son is dead!"

"I swear I didn't mean for shit to go down like that" Marvin said. "I came up here to see if you had any soldiers out on the streets that I could team up with so I can go get Nancy back."

Ali could see how much Marvin cared for Nancy just from him talking, and it made him sick to his stomach. How dare he come up here asking for help. Ali quickly reached over the table, and snuffed Marvin out of his seat. He then jumped on top of Marvin, and started raining blows on his exposed face until several C.O.'s came over and tackled Ali to the floor and piled up on him. "Stay the fuck away from Nancy mufucka!" Ali screamed as the C.O.'s roughly escorted him out of the visiting room.

When Marvin walked out of the prison Moonie sat behind the wheel of the Benz they rode in. "How'd it go?"

Marvin sighed loudly. "Not good...looks like we going to have to take this bitch Pauleena down ourselves" Pauleena had wiped out most of Marvin's soldiers. All Marvin had left were a bunch of petty thugs, and Moonie. He hated to admit it, but he didnt have enough fire power to go head up with Pauleena anymore.

* * *

Pauleena laid across her king sized bed wearing nothing but a sky blue thong. When she was home she liked to be comfortable and free. Pauleena sipped on a glass of wine as she thought about what she was going to do with Nancy's body once she had her killed. Just as Pauleena was getting comfortable she saw Romelo's car pulled up in her drive way in her security cameras. "Fuck does this clown want" Pauleena sucked her teeth, as she got up, and covered her body with a silk robe.

Pauleena entered the living room bare foot, with her glass of wine in her hand. She smiled at the nervous look that Romelo plastered on his face. She loved to see the look of fear on people's faces. "How can I help you?" She asked in a bored tone.

"I'm here to put an end to all this madness" Romelo stood to his feet. "I don't want to have to bury my son."

"That sounds like a personal problem to me" Pauleena said slowly sipping her wine. "You think I give a flying fuck about your son?"

"Listen" Romelo raised his voice. "I'm asking you end this for me. I never wanted this to start from the beginning."

Pauleena chuckled. "You wanna know what's so funny? Is that if I was losing this war, and your son was the one winning it, would you still be standing in my living room right now?" With that being said Pauleena removed a gun from one of her Muslim security guard waist band.

"Don't do this Pauleena" Romelo begged. "I didn't come here for this."

"Yes you did" Pauleena said as she fired two shots into Romelo's chest. She watched him drop to the floor like a sack of potatoes and clutch his stomach. She stood there and watched until Romelo stopped moving.

"Clean this shit up" Pauleena said as she headed downstairs to the basement.

Nancy sat tied to a chair sitting in the basement, her mouth covered by several layers of duct tape. Her head snapped in the direction where she heard foot steps. She looked up and saw Pauleena walking towards her.

"You hungry?" Pauleena asked. Nancy nodded her head yes.

"I'll have my chef bring you something to eat in a second" Pauleena said roughly snatching the tape from off of Nancy's lips. "If you scream imma put the tape back on."

"Thank you" Nancy whispered.

"Dont mention it" Pauleena winked at her before she disapeared back up the stairs. The first chance Nancy got she planned on killing Pauleena, she couldn't stand her and wanted to see her beg for her life. But for right now all she could do was sit and wait.

* * *

When Marvin got news about what had happend
to his father he went crazy. He tore his house up
from top to bottom breaking any, and everything
that was breakable. He burried his head in his
hands, and just cried his eyes out. Marvin wanted
Pauleena dead so bad he could taste it. He got up,
grabbed his gun and headed out the door in search
of her.

"WHAT WOULD YOU DO?"

Coco had set up a nice funeral several for Lil Ali, it was the least she could do especially since she felt like she wasn't there for her best friend when she needed her the most. Coco just prayed that where ever Nancy was that she was still alive and breathing. Nancy didn't deal with too many people so only a few females were there. Everybody else was all Ali's people. Several goons stood around the funeral home looking suspicious. Skip stood over in the corner having a word with Loco and a few members from his organization. No one hadn't seen or heard from Loco ever since his girlfriend Monique had been gunned down in their home.

Coco couldn't control the tears that streamed down her face. Not once did she go over and look at Lil Ali's body. She just couldn't do it, that would of been too much for her. The entire funeral home got quiet when Ali stepped foot in the place shackled from his hands down to his ankles. Three chunky looking C.O.'s escorted him inside the place.

"Yo what's good?" Ali said to one of the C.O.'s nodding towards the cuffs that were tightly wrapped around his wrist. The C.O. removed the cuffs from Ali's wrist, but his ankles were still shackled together. Ali looked down at his son's little lifeless body and pale face and broke down crying. What kind of animal could just kill a child in cold blood like it was nothing? Ali didn't know Pauleena, but he definitely planned on getting to know her very well. Just as the C.O. was about to place the hand cuffs back on Ali the doors to the funeral home busted open and in ran Marvin and Moonie both carrying machine guns. They both wore hoodies with a bandana covering the bottom half of their face. "Dont fucking move!" Marvin yelled.

Skip, and Loco calmly walked up to C.O.'s and hand cuffed them with they own cuffs. They watched as one of their three hundred pound goons scooped Ali up, and tossed him over his shoulder quickly escorting him out of the funeral home, and into the van that awaited them curb side. Marvin, Moonie, Skip, and Loco all ran out the funeral home and hopped in the back of the vanr just before it peeled off.

"I appreciate it" Ali said as Marvin removed the shackles from his ankle. Ali was happy to finally be back on the streets, but he knew every police officer and federal agent would be trying to hunt him down within the next few hours. He would deal with that bridge when it was time to cross it. Right now his focus was getting Nancy back and finding Pauleena.

"What we doing first?" Skip asked.

Ali looked over at Skip, and shook his head. "Yo stop the van" he ordered. When the van came to a stop Ali opened up the door. "Get the fuck outta here."

"You know I can't just leave you like that" Skip replied.

"You have a family to take care of" Ali reminded him. "You put in more than enough work already...now I need you to get out this van, and go home....please!"

Skip sat there and thought about it for a second, before he gave Ali a hug, and hopped out the van and watched as it pulled off.

"We gon need as many men as we can get if we expect to take Pauleena down" Marvin said.

"I'll find us another man, just not Skip" Ali said. He'd seen a lot of hustlers die out in the streets and he wouldn't be able to forgive himself if anything happened to Skip. If anybody deserved a happy ending it was him.

"SLOW DOWN"

Pauleena and Paco sat in her office watching the news. They listened to the reporter explain how Ali had escaped the guards at the funeral home. She knew the reason behind Ali's breakout and she also knew exactly where he was headed.

"He must really love that bimbo down in the basement" Paco chuckled. He had heard about Ali and his crew making noise out in the streets a few years ago. "You know he's going to be gunning for you cause you killed his son right?"

"I'll be ready" Pauleena smiled. Once she heard the news that Ali had escaped she knew her house would more than likely be his first stop. "That mufucka can come here if he wants to" she laughed out loud.

"I say you just let me go down to the basement, and kill that raggedy bitch" Paco suggested. He wasn't into playing games. His job was to kill people, and that's what he did best.

"Nah I want to see if this Nigga really got enough balls to come to my house and try to save this chick, this I gotta see" Pauleena laughed. To her this was all a game, and whoever was the last hustler standing was the winner.

* * *

Marvin parked his smoke black Dodge Camaro in a well known strip club parking lot. He had got word that Knowledge was inside tricking off with a few Spanish chicks. Just as the two men was about to hop out the car they spotted Knowledge leaving the club with two chicks on his arm.

"There he go right there" Ali said spotting him immediately. "Pull up right next to that Nigga."

Knowledge strolled through the parking lot talking shit to the two women, who smiled and laughed at everything he said even if it wasn't funny. All that was on Knowledge's mind was all the sexual things he planned on doing with the women. As Knowledge strolled through the parking lot he felt a car creeping up behind him, off instincts he gripped the handle of his .45.

The Camaro pulled up on the side of him, and the passenger window rolled down. Ali stuck his head out the window along with his P89. "What up!" he said and opened fire. POW, POW, POW, POW!!

Once Knowledge saw Ali's face he already knew what time it was. He quickly pushed one of the women into the Camaro as he took off running in the opposite direction firing reckless shots over his shoulder. Knowledge zig zagged through several parked cars hunched down so he would be out of the killer's site.

"Fuck!" Knowledge cursed as he stayed low and caught his breath. At this moment he knew it was either kill or be killed. He quickly sprinted over towards his Range Rover. Knowledge pulled out into the streets like a mad man. He peeked in the rearview mirror and saw the Camaro right behind him. Knowledge made a quick left and merge onto the highway where he gunned the engine. Within seconds he was easily going past 100 mph.

"Hold on" Ali said as he reached in the back seat, and grabbed the Tec-9 that rested on the seat. "Okay now I'm ready."

Marvin stomped on the gas pedal, as the Camaro's engine roared quickly picking up speed. Ali hung halfway out the window with his Tec-9 in his hand as the Camaro gained chase on the Range Rover. Once the Camaro was close enough Ali aimed his gun down at the Range Rover's tires and pulled the trigger. He and Marvin watched as the Range Rover lost control, and flipped over at least twenty times before crashing into a tree. "One down and one more to go" Ali said leaning back in his seat. Anyone that had something to do with his son being killed was on his hitlist.

"THE LAST HUSTLER STANDING"

Ali strapped on his bullet proof vest as he watched the rest of his soldiers prepare to fight what might be their last battle. He appreciated how many people still believed in him enough to risk their lives for him. All that was on his mind was killing Pauleena and getting Nancy back in one piece.

"Today is the day" Marvin smiled clutching his A.K. "Promise me you'll let me kill that bitch."

"Whoever gets to her first" Ali said dryly. He still didn't really care for Marvin especially since he was trying to fuck his fiance. He tried to push the thoughts of him, and Nancy to back of his mind cause right now he needed as many soldiers as he could get.

"Ya'll better just hope I don't run into that bitch first" Moonie huffed.

"So whats the plan?" Loco asked.

"We going to run straight up in Pauleena's house" Ali said with a serious murderous look on his face. Ali and his team hopped in three separate vans, each one following the other to Pauleena's house.

* * *

Pauleena sat in her office staring a hole through her lawyer. Young Jeezy's mix tape "The Real Is Back" flowed through the speakers at a reasonable tone. She listened as her greedy lawyer tried to milk her out of more money for the charges that Detective Nelson had placed on her. Pauleena hated to be taken advantage of, but she kept quiet until the lawyer was finished speaking. "So what you telling me is to make this case go away it's going to take $200,000?"

"That's only if I can bribe the judge with that" he paused. "Might be a little more....I have to grease a lot of palms."

Pauleena laughed as she removed one of her 9mm from the holster under her arm. "Are you fucking with me?"

"No.....no you know I wouldn't do something like that" the lawyer answered in a shaky voice.

"You are going to make this charge go away" she told him. "And you're going to do it for $100,000."

"I'm afraid that's impossible" the lawyer said as beads of sweat began to form on his forehead.

"Either you make this charge go away for $100,000....or I make you go away for way less than that the choice is yours" Pauleena said waiting for a response.

"I'll get started on your case first thing in the morning" the lawyer said nervously.

"That's what I thought you would say" Pauleena smiled placing her gun back in its holster. Before she could say another word one of her Muslim security guards came busting into her office out of breath.

"Boss....we got trouble look at your surveillance cameras!" The Muslim's voice boomed. Pauleena, Paco, and the lawyer all looked over at the flat screen and saw several men wearing all black carrying assault rifles running across her front lawn heading for the front door.

"I knew he would be coming" Pauleena smiled. "Strap up!"

Loco ran up to the front door, shot the lock off, and barged inside. One of Pauleena's Muslim body guards waited on the other side of the door holding a shotgun. Once Loco came running in the house the Muslim pulled the trigger sending him right back out the front door head first. BOOOOOOOM!!!!

Once Ali saw Loco body come flying back out the front door, he quickly fired his Tec-9 at the big man as him, and the rest of his crew entered the mansion. Ali and Marvin quickly got into a shootout with the rest of Pauleena's security.

Silk White

Nancy rested tied down to the chair sleeping when a loud burst of gunfire woke her up out of her sleep. She didn't know what was going on, but she figured it was Marvin coming to save her.

Pauleena didn't know what was going on downstairs but from the sound of it, somebody would of thought a world war was going on.

"What's going on down there...?" The lawyer asked with a scared look on his face. Pauleena didn't reply, instead she pulled out her 9mm and put a bullet in the lawyers head, she was tired of hearing him talk. Pauleena took off the jacket to the all white suit she wore and kicked off her heels. She threw her hair in a ponytail as she walked over to the closet where she kept all of her guns. Pauleena grabbed two Tec-9's from the closet and exited her office to join the gun fight. Once Pauleena stepped out into the hallway she immediately filled three of the gunmen with lead. She walked throughout her house barefoot, looking for Ali.

Ali slowly crept upstairs in search of Nancy. He cautiously took baby steps as he searched several rooms looking for Nancy. As Ali exited one of the rooms he spotted Pauleena at the end of the hall. The two locked eyes. They both raised their guns at the same time and squeezed the trigger. Four bullets hit Ali's vest dropping off impact. Pauleena quickly dived down the steps dodging Ali's bullets by a fingernail. Pauleena tumbled all the way down to the bottom of the steps. "Shit!" she laid on her back looking at the ceiling wincing in pain. As she laid on floor, she noticed she no longer heard gun shots. She looked around, and saw dead bodies everywhere, some wore all black, while the others were her Muslim security. When Pauleena finally made it to her feet she looked up, and saw Moonie standing in front of her with a gun aimed at her chest.

"Bitch didn't I tel, you I was gon kill Yo dumb ass!?" Moonie growled.

"Bitch please you ain't gon do shit" Pauleena said flicking her wrist dismissively. "I'll die a boss, and you'll always be a bum."

Moonie bit down on her bottom lip as she pulled the trigger on gun. CLICK! She looked down at the revolver, and cursed.

Pauleena laughed. "You done fucked up now bitch" she said putting her hands up signaling it was time to fight. Moonie tossed the empty gun to the floor, as she ran, and charged Pauleena. The two fought like wild animals, each one trying to kill the other with each swing.

* * *

Ali laid on the floor holding his chest. He knew for a fact that one of his ribs was broken. Just as he tried to get up he felt a foot kick him in his face. Paco stood over Ali with a wicked smirk on his face. Ali struggled to his feet and looked over at the crazy looking man who held a hunting knife in his hand. Paco took a swipe at Ali causing him to jump back. "Don't run you pussy" Paco said in a heavy accent stepping a little closer. Paco lunged at Ali trying to jab the hunting knife in his stomach. Ali quickly side stepped out the way, as he watched the knife get stuck in the wall. Ali caught Paco with a quick two piece causing him to stumble backwards. Paco quickly rushed Ali as the two went crashing over through the balcony all the way down to the living room. Paco landed awkwardly on his neck and died instantly. Ali landed on his back, his head bounced off the floor like a basketball knocking him out cold.

* * *

Marvin searched each room in the entire house looking for Nancy. The only place he hadn't searched was down stairs. When Marvin made it downstairs he heard a lot of commotion coming from the two women fighting. He paid them two no mind as he spotted a door which looked like it lead down to the basement.

When Nancy saw Marvin come downstairs her eyes lit up with joy. She had never been more happy to see someone. "I'm glad to see you."

"I'm happy to see you too baby" Marvin said as he quickly cut Nancy loose. He lifted Nancy up his arms rushing to get her away from all this madness.

* * *

Pauleena and Moonie continued to go blow for blow as the fight spilled into the kitchen. When Moonie began getting the better of Pauleena she quickly reached on the counter for a knife. Moonie was punching Pauleena with all of her might when out of nowhere she felt a sharp pain pierce through her stomach. Moonie grabbed at her stomach, and looked confused when she looked down at her bloody hands. Pauleena quickly hopped up, and plunged the kitchen knife in and out of Moonie's body at least thirty times before she stopped.

"Stupid bitch!" Pauleena huffed as she hopped off Moonie's dead body. When Pauleena turned around she stood face to face with Ali. Before she could say a word. Ali slapped her across her face with his P89 knocking her unconscious. Ali stood over Pauleena about to fire when he heard a familiar voice coming from behind him. Ali looked behind him, and saw Marvin carrying Nancy in his arms like the two had just gotten married.

"Oh my God Ali!" Nancy yelled in excitement as she hopped out of Marvin's arms, and ran full speed jumping in Ali's arms. "Oh my God I missed you so much daddy!" As the two kissed passionately.

Marvin cleared his throat to get Ali's and Nancy's attention. It made him sick to his stomach to see Nancy kiss another man even though she wasn't his girl. "I think we should get out of here before the cops......." POW!

Ali raised his armed, and put a bullet right between Marvin's eyes silencing him forever. At the end of the day it was still Marvin's fault why Little Ali was no longer alive. If he hadn't gone to Nancy's house Ali's son would still be alive. Nancy didn't want to see Marvin get killed, but in her heart she knew he had to go.

"That's for that clown letting our son get killed, andthen running off leaving you for dead" Ali said dropping the gun to the floor.

"I missed you sooooooo much" Nancy said as she and Ali began kissing like wild animals. Ali gently laid Nancy on her back, as he crept in between her legs, literally ripping her panties off. The first thing he did was taste his sweet pussy that he had missed so much. Nancy moaned loudly as she pushed his head away. She pushed Ali on his back, and quickly straddled him. She badly needed to feel her dick. When Ali entered her walls Nancy moaned loudly. They started out slow, but then they went at it. Nancy bounced up, and down on Ali's dick riding it like a porno star forcing him cum inside of her. When the two were done, they both laid on the floor breathing heavily. Nancy quickly jumped up when she heard movement coming from the kitchen.

Pauleena stumbled out the kitchen. She was still drowsy from the blow to the head that she took. When Nancy saw her she took off running in her direction. Nancy tackled Pauleena and proceeded to beat her face in with her fist until it was a bloodly mess. Ali walked over and handed Nancy his P89.

Nancy stood to her feet with the gun aimed down at Pauleena's head. Her hands shook uncontrollably. She so badly wanted to blow her brains out, but for some reason she just couldn't do it. "Bitch you not even worth it!" Nancy huffed as she lifted her leg and stomped Pauleena in the face one last time. "Come on baby let's get outta here before the cops come."

Ali gave Nancy one last hug before he, and Nancy exited the house. As soon as they stepped outside they both could already hear the sirens not too far away. Ali, and Nancy quickly hopped in Pauleena's 600 Benz luckily for them the keys were left in the ignition. Ali backed out the drive way and sped down the street.

* * *

Pauleena scrambled to her feet still a little dizzy. She ran upstairs to her room and filled up two duffle bags with as much money as she could, before escaping out the back door where she kept her black Lexus parked for situations like this. Pauleena hopped in the Lexus and peeled off. She didn't know what state she was headed to, but wherever she was headed was far from NEW YORK.

* * *

"Where we going?" Nancy asked.

"Somewhere safe for the night" Ali answered quickly. "I got $150,000 in a safety deposit box, we gon go get that tomorrow, then hit the road... I don't know where we going yet, but we getting the fuck up outta here!"

"Thank you for coming to save me baby" Nancy said as tears streamed down her face. "Nobody has ever loved me the way you do."

"You would of did the same for me" Ali said noticing flashing lights in the rearview mirror. "Hold on!" He yelled making a sharp left causing the car to fishtail. Nancy looked behind her, and couldn't believe how many cop cars were behind them. Ali gunned the engine pushing the car to its speed limit. The Benz zoomed passed car after car weaving its way through the minor traffic. "All we gotta do is reach the highway, and we good" Ali said keeping his eyes on the road.

"Ah shit" Nancy huffed when she saw the helicopter flying in the sky above them. Right then, and there she knew that they weren't going to getaway. Ali zoomed through the intersection avoiding a major cullision by an inch or two. When the Benz reached the ramp that lead to the highway it was block off by several police cars.

"Shit!!" Ali cursed as he stomped on the breaks, causing the Benz to a skidding, screetching stop. Several police cars quickly surrounded the Benz.

"What are we going to do?" Nancy asked in a panic tone.

"Get out!" Ali told her. "Go get that $150,000 and live the rest of your life stress free, I don't know if meeting you was a gift or a curse."

"Are you crazy!?" Nancy yelled. "I'm not leaving you!"

"You have to baby" Ali said as silent tears rolled down his face. "I can't go back to jail"

"And being without you is like jail for me, and I can't go back to jail either!" Nancy said trying to hold back her tears but she couldn't.

"Step out the car with your hands up!!" An officer said through the intercom of his squad car. "There's nowhere for you to run."

"Get out the fucking car!" Ali yelled.

"Nooo!" Nancy yelled back. "I'm not leaving you, if I can't be with you, then I rather be dead away."

"You sure you wanna do this?" Ali asked leaning over to kiss Nancy.

"I'm positive baby" Nancy smiled. "I love you!"

"I love you too baby" Ali replied as he reached out and held Nancy's hand.

"We ride together and we gon die together" Nancy smiled. Ali took a deep breath, as he shifted the gear back in drive. "You ready baby?"

"Let's do it!"

Ali turned the radio up as loud as it would go, as he, and Nancy bobbed their Head's to the beat that blasted throughout the speakers. Ali leaned over and kissed Nancy on last time as he stomped on the gas pedal. Bullets riddled and rocked the Benz from side to side as Ali drove straight through the road block. Bullets made loud pinging noises as they bounced off the Benz until it finally came to a stop. Inside Ali's head rested on the steering wheel, while Nancy's head rested on the dash board by the glove compartment. The first officer on the scene opened the Benz door, and saw that Ali, and Nancy were dead, but they were still holding hands. When the paramedics finally removed Ali and Nancy from the car they were surprised to see that the two both died with a smile on their bloody faces.

***

Coco cried her eyes out as she listened to the reporter report that she had just lost her best friend. Inside she felt bad. Coco knew if she was there she would of definately died right along with them. Coco cut the TV off and headed upstairs where she planned on trying to sleep through the pain of losing the only family she ever had.

Books by Good2Go Authors

Coming Soon

On Our Bookshelf

Good2Go Films Presents

To order films please go to www.good2gofilms.com
To order books, please fill out the order form below:

Name:

_____

Address:

_____

_____

City: _____ State: _____ Zip Code: _____

_____

Phone:

_____

Email:

_____

Method Payment:

Check   VISA   ☐   MASTERCARD   ☐

Credit Card#:

_____

Name as it appears on card:

_____

Signature:

_____

Item Name	Price	Qty	Amount
He Loves Me, He Loves You Not - Mychea	$13.95		
He Loves Me, He Loves You Not 2 - Mychea	$13.95		
Married To Da Streets – Silk White	$13.95		
Never Be The Same – Silk White	$13.95		
Tears of a Hustler - Silk White	$13.95		
Tears of a Hustler 2 - Silk White	$13.95		
Tears of a Hustler 3 - Silk White	$13.95		
Tears of a Hustler 4- Silk White	$13.95		
The Teflon Queen – Silk White	$13.95		
The Teflon Queen 2 – Silk White	$13.95		
Young Goonz – Reality Way	$13.95		
Subtotal:			
Tax:			

Shipping (Free) U.S. Media Mail:			
Total:			

Make Checks Payable To:
Good2Go Publishing
7311 W Glass Lane
Laveen, AZ 85339

CPSIA information can be obtained at www.ICGtesting.com
Printed in the USA
LVOW10s1541010616

490797LV00021B/765/P